Praise for Aaron M. Wilson

"Wilson's perfectly plotted stories engross their readers in a world where environmental concerns are paramount. His characters are unafraid to fight for their ideals, and yet they retain a humanity that allows readers to identify with them, which illustrates his penchant for carefully crafted fiction."

- Darci Schummer, author & poet

"Thoughtful, insightful, and intuitive: readers will share in a book that decodes the human condition."

- Hunter Liguore, author of *The Forsakens* & the
editor of *The Last Man Anthology*

"A narrative that careens through space & time, *The Many Lives of Inez Wick* brings us serious environmental issues in a swirl of hard-bitten fragments—Edward Abbey meets Quentin Tarantino."

- John Hayes, author of *The Spring Ghazals*

"Wilson has a way of writing that lets him transparently share his passion for environmentalism while entertaining us with a vivid plot and this collection of shorts displays his talent marvelously."

- M. Chase Whittemore, editor of Evolve Journal

THE MANY LIVES OF INEZ WICK

AARON M. WILSON

An Everything Feeds Process Press Book

The Many Lives of Inez Wick

by Aaron M. Wilson

"The Bike Mechanic" was previously published by *Soulless Machine* as part of *Tuesday Serial* managed by P.J Kaiser, 1 June 2010 through 12 October 2010.

"No Compromise" has been accepted to be published in *Girls with Guns Anthology* edited by Tonya Moore & Made in DNA.

"Dog Fight" was previously published by *Pow Fast Flash Fiction* edited by Karen Schindler, 25 April 2010.

"Beyond Peaking: Chapter One" was previously published by *Writers Talk* edited by John Hayes 16 September 2010 and *The Hive Mind* edited by Alexandra Wolf, 18 June 2010.

"*Apophis*" was previously published by *eFiction Magazine: The Premier Internet Fiction Magazine* edited by Doug Lance, 2 September 2010.

"Spilling Sunlight" was previously published by *Evolve Journal* edited by M. Chase Whittemore, 2 August 2010.

ISBN: 0615438229

ISBN-13: 9780615438221

Library of Congress Control Number: 2011920433

Published by Everything Feeds Process Press, Minneapolis, MN

PLEASE NOTE

Acknowledgements

First, I would like to thank Jessica Fox-Wilson, talented poet, author of *Blameless Mouth*, editor, best friend and wife. With her love and support, I feel that anything is possible.

Secondly, I'd like to thank my writers group for the encouragement and deadlines without which these stories wouldn't have been finished: Darci Schummer, Michele Campbell, Todd Wardrope, Judy Johnson, Matt Johnson, and Jessica Fox-Wilson. You are inspirational in your support of my work and in the dedication to your own creative ventures.

Third, I'd like to thank Bob Lipski – author and illustrator of *Uptown Girl* – for creating the book cover. Without the motivation I received from your art, I just don't think I would have finished.

Fourth, I'd like to thank the online community of writers that have taken interest in my fiction, given some of it a home, and motivated me to keep typing: P.J. Kaiser, Karen Schindler, Doug Lance, M. Chase Whittemore, Tonya Moore, Hunter Liguore, Alexandra Wolfe, John Hayes, Jim Wisneski, and all those who tweet and re-tweet with me.

Lastly, I'd like to thank my parents for teaching me to pursue what makes me happy and that a "job" is something that you do to support your dreams.

For

Jessica Fox-Wilson, my loving wife, my best friend, my creative partner, and my so much more…

Table of Contents

Stories

"Women are supposed to be very calm generally: but women feel just as men feel; they need exercise for their faculties, and a field for their efforts as much as their brothers do; they suffer from too rigid a restraint, too absolute a stagnation, precisely as men would suffer; and it is narrow-minded in their more privileged fellow-creatures to say that they ought to confine themselves to making puddings and knitting stockings, to playing on the piano and embroidering bags."

–Charlotte Bronte, Jane Eyre

Author's Preface

Some may say that we humans only get one chance to invent ourselves, one life to live. What if we were able to see a timeline of our lives, an older self looking back over the important moments – decisions – of our younger lives? Would we make the same choices, go down the same roads? Or, would we take alternative paths?

Inez Wick has many lives. Her main timeline begins in the story "Spilling Sunlight," in which her life is changed forever, haunted by greasy flames. All the timelines begin with the last story in the collection, which hopefully shines a light on her motivations when, as a reader, you'll needed it most.

Form that transformative moment, Inez goes off to college. In college, she becomes a super heroine of sorts, in "Lady Aqua," fighting against despoilers of the natural world. Here there is a branch: 1) she either gets caught or 2) she escapes.

1) Having been caught, Inez is thrust into the deadly adventure where she'll meet a mysterious man going by the name Daniel Emmett Seward in "The Bike Mechanic" and ultimately end up in a pit fighting for her life in "Dogfight."

2) Having escaped, Inez is free to continue the good fight, which takes her to a China where the air is too toxic to breathe in "No Compromise."

Both options 1 and 2 end poorly for Inez, so what would her life look like if she made different decisions while in college or before she went off to college?

Perhaps instead of studying the environment and becoming a radical activist, she 3) chose to study astronomy as in the story "*Apophis.*" And perhaps, stranger still, let's assume that the traumatic event in "Spilling Sunlight" never happened and 4) her mother and father live to see retirement as in the story "Beyond Peaking."

I think that it is only human to look back at decisions we have made and either regret them fully or wonder what might have been down another path. Inez Wick never hesitates in the moment. She is a woman who is strong in her convictions. Once she has started down a chosen path, she commits to it. She believes in her work. Only the reader is privy to the possible alternatives, and it is up to the reader to decide which of *The Many Lives of Inez Wick* is her true fate.

Aaron M. Wilson, 2011

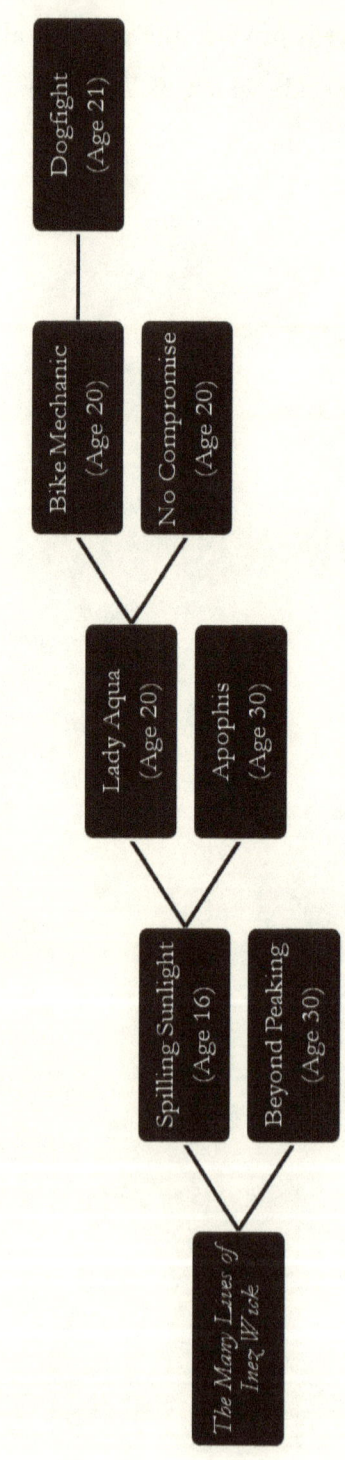

The Many Lives of Inez Wick

The Bike Mechanic

One

Dan Seward stood behind the display counter with tire levers in both hands, admiring the bent rims, broken spokes, and flat tires on the mountain bike he had up on his work stand. He yawned, thinking that it was too early to be up. His customers wouldn't be up for several hours yet, so why did he think that opening by eight every day was a good idea? He huffed, "It just feels right to work in the morning." His father and mother had always been out the door before six, which was something that Seward had always promised he would never submit himself to for very long. Yet, here he was, hard at work before sunrise, enjoying almost every minute. Despite loving the work, he missed the old days and longed for the excitement that only C4-activism could elicit.

Slipping the tire levers between the rim and the tire's sidewalls, Seward slowly bent and twisted the tires off without pinching the inner tube. Even though he liked the simplicity of a hard tail, there were times and places for full or at least half suspension bikes. Looking at the abuse that the mountain bike had taken, he was sure that the owner had bitten off more than the bike could chew.

Seward tried to imagine what the rider looked like: athletic but not fit, soft round the middle but not overweight, and likely tan but fake tanned; after the accident that did in the bike, the rider was also likely bruised, scraped, and lucky to have only bent up the bike's rims. However, the work ticket on the bike didn't have any clues. It was just the usual: "Scrap if repair exceeds value." Most people didn't try Seward's Custom Cycle Repair & Junk Yard first. They'd try the high end places first like Erik's with clean, well-spaced and orderly displays, helpful sales people, and overnight service. Customers wouldn't find such niceties at Seward's.

At Seward's, customers were encouraged to fix their own bikes. Seward had started the shop to fulfill his required community service hours, doing something that he felt gave back to the community and had some sustaining potential for the future. The shop was more like a garage that was sectioned off into several fully equipped workstations. Customers could rent a station by the hour and make use of any and all of Seward's tools. There were also buckets of parts that could be scavenged, nothing more than five or ten dollars in any of them. He'd salvaged the parts from bikes like the one he was working on now, when the owner decided that the cost of repair was just shy of something newer and shinier.

It was sad. Most people were only willing to shell out a couple hundred for a bike, which meant they were buying inferior parts. For most people – people who didn't off road – those bikes were adequate. However, when someone took a two-hundred dollar Wal-Mart special, like this one off road, even though it was from a quality name brand like Specialized, the bike usually end up in Seward's shop or as parts. Seward had unsuccessfully tried to explain that to a few customers by sarcastically asking if they'd feel safe taking a Yugo off road.

After more closely inspecting the bike, Seward decided to call the customer and deliver the bad news: his labor to true the rims and straighten the front and rear dropouts would likely exceed the cost of the bike. As he went to take the bike down off his work stand, the front door chimed. In rolled a Big Dummy: the very popular Surly model with an extend frame that allowed for a rider to haul a hell of a lot of stuff in two oversized panniers. Big Dummies were very popular with the outdoor types that liked to camp, eat granola, and smoke more than their fair share of weed.

Seward looked up from the bike to the owner pushing the Big Dummy in through the door. She was a beauty out of a Bike Magazine fantasy: tall, fit, tan, raven black hair cut into a bob with blue poking out from underneath around the back of her neck. Her arms were bare and covered in a chaotic rainbow of tattoos: flowering vines that laced and tangled their way around her arms.

Suddenly, Seward felt like he had woken up in a Raymond Chandler noir, and he found himself thinking that she was going to be nothing but trouble.

Two

She leaned the Big Dummy against a wall, opened up one of the panniers and pulled out a multi-tool and a half-eaten sandwich. After taking a bite of the sandwich, she rummaged through the pile of fenders.

Seward picked up a flyer, what he liked to think as the Seward Custom Repair Shop's Menu of Services, and he made his way over. He held out the flyer. "What can I help you with?" He would have rather given her a pick up line, but he needed money. Even in the current economy, people still tended to buy new bikes rather than used ones or parts. Plus, the rent on the building was due again in a few days.

Looking Seward in the eyes, she took the flyer. "I've got a long haul ahead. I was just passing by when I saw your sign. Thought I'd take a look around." She handed the flyer back. "I think that I'd like to use your bathroom, and…" She looked over Seward's shoulder, "I might make use of a station."

Seward shrugged his shoulders. "Five dollars an hour. Plus parts and lube." He walked back to the counter and picked up a key. He held it up. "Key for the bathroom. There's a shower back there. Feel free to use it." He knew she'd been on the road a while by her offending odors, a mixture of damp earth, freshly cut grass, and earthworms after a thunderstorm. Normally, Seward found sweaty women all the more attractive, but she smelled spoiled.

"Really?" She opened the other pannier and pulled out some clothes. "You have a towel?"

Seward had stocked towels when he opened, but found that he hated laundry day more since then, so he stopped. "Sorry, no. However, there are a couple bars of soap and some cheap shampoo." He bunched up his face as if tasting something bitter. "If you feel so inclined, there's a 'Support Me' jar back there. If you can spare anything to help keep it stocked, it'd be much appreciated."

As she hurried by, keeping her head down, she said, "Thanks, Emmet."

At hearing his middle name said aloud, Seward's typical relaxed demeanor was replaced with one of panicked curiosity.

Emmet, he thought. *No one round here knows me as Emmet. No one beside my parole-officer, and I haven't had to see him in a couple of years.*

His thoughts kept spinning round and round until he landed on the last time he'd used his middle name. It'd been more than ten years, back when he'd been in college in Michigan. At that time, he'd thought that he'd been Dan in high school, so in college he'd wanted to see where Emmet would get him. Funny thing, Emmet didn't get him very far. Sounded too Southern, and Northern folk equate Southern with slow and stupid.

Well, he thought, *pondering wouldn't pay the bills.* He picked up the next ticket and found a real rock-jumper that needed suspension work. He took the bike from his lined up orders and placed it on his work stand. As he lifted the bike, the suspension fork dropped to its full extension.

After securing the bike, he applied pressure to the front tire to test the suspension. The fork easily slid all the way up as if there wasn't air in them. *First things first*, he thought as he collected an air pump. He opened the damping valve and attempted to re-pressurize the fork, but after a few pumps, he realized that the seals were blown, and he'd have to take the suspension apart and rebuild it with new seals. Lucky for the customer, Seward kept replacement seals on hand. They were hard to come by because the manufacturer would rather have the sale of a new fork for $1,600 than four-dollar replacement seals. And so would most retailers for that matter, while Seward just wanted to get people back on the road and out of their cars.

Seward put all of his focus into repairing the suspension fork, but in between steps, his mind drifted to the woman using the shop's shower. Other than her off putting odor, she was attractive. He couldn't escape imagining her naked body. He bet she'd have more tattoos than those on her arms. Those thoughts led him to imaging her opening the door to the shower and inviting him to join her. However, she had known Seward's middle name, and his acute sense of self-preservation trumped fantasy.

Before he knew it, he'd pressurized the suspension fork, taken the bike down off of his work stand, and parked it with the others ready for pick up. He was about to call and leave a message for the bike's owner as the woman came out from the shower drying her hair with a t-shirt.

"Thanks. I really needed a shower." She put down five bucks on the counter. "For the workspace for the next hour." She packed her clothes back and rolled her bike over to the station furthest from the shop's windows.

Seward watched her for a few minutes as she tinkered, tightening a few bolts and checking her tire alignment before going back to his pile of repairs. He wanted to know how she knew his middle name. He walked over to her workstation.

He wasn't one to beat around the bush, so he asked her outright. "How do you know my middle name?"

She put her tools down slowly and turned around. Her eyes were wide.

"I mean, no one round here knows me as Emmet. I go by Dan or Seward." He held out his hand to her and smiled. "Hi. I'm Dan Seward."

His awkward backpedaling must have lightened the mood because she took his hand and replied, "I'm Inez."

Seward let go of her hand. "So, Inez…" He let the question trail off as he looked at her bike. "What do you think of the Big Dummy?"

"It's a little heavy, but it's the station wagon of hybrid bikes."

Seward nodded. "I like to think of them as SUVs."

"Manlier." She put her hands on her hips. "Either way, they get the job done."

"Yeah. That they do."

Inez still looked nervous, but as her shoulder's sagged, she opened up. "You're Daniel Emmet Seward." She looked around as if to check for eavesdroppers. "You're the environmentalist who took out the lumber mill a few years back near Ann Arbor." Inez paused. "I was told you might still be sympathetic to the cause – that you might help me."

Three

"I run a bicycle junk yard," Seward crossed his arms defensively and took a step back. "Look around." He was going to elaborate on the ecological value of recycling bicycles and getting people out of their cars, but didn't want to get sidetracked, "So, you know who I am. I'd like to know who told you where to find me?"

Inez put the wrench in her hand down on the counter before meeting his eyes. "Al sent me."

"The fuck he did." Seward quickly looked around the shop. It was still empty except for the two of them. He turned and walked to the front door, flipped OPEN to CLOSED, and locked it. He picked up a seat post still connected to a ratty looking saddle and slowly walked back over her workstation.

Seward looked quickly to the early morning street though the display windows. The streets were will empty. He raised his improvised club. "You have until ten to give me the safe word before I feed you to my compost heap." He looked back out at the street. "One, two, three, four…"

Inez didn't seem to be frightened. The only sign that seemed to indicate that she was taking Seward's threat seriously was that she had taken two steps backward and had her back up against the worktable.

"…five, six…" Seward was ready. He wasn't going to let past mistakes ruin what he had going here. His life wasn't perfect. He was always strapped for cash, and some weeks he had to go without a few meals, but he was his own boss. He also felt that he was doing the local community a service by giving teens a place to hangout and work on their bikes after school and on the weekends. "…seven, eight…"

Inez reached into her pocket and pulled out a small laminated card with a clenched fist in a circle, lines radiating out from the fist. She held it up and read the word on the back, *Hayduke*. She held out the card for Seward to take. "Really, Edward Abbey? Seems, I don't know, cliché."

Seward wasn't sure he wanted to put the seat post down. He looked at her bike and for a split second thought that he could get away with killing her and make a tidy profit. Instead, he shook his head and dropped seat post at his feet. "That person is long gone. I haven't been Emmet Seward in over fifteen years."

Seward took the card. "Wow. Earth First." Seward rolled up his sleeve exposing a tattoo that matched the emblem on the card. Then he opened his hand indicating that she should look around the shop. "My activism these days is what you see here."

Inez looked around. "I like it."

"So," Seward rolled his sleeve back down. "Why do you need Emmet Seward?"

Four

Inez retrieved a map. She spoke as she walked across the shop to the sales counter. "The University of Michigan's chapter of The Monkey Wrench Gang is still active. We're still under your original charter. Did you really write the charter as a freshman?" Inez opened a map of Northern Michigan and flattened it out on the glass counter top.

Seward listened. He didn't want to believe that the student club he started his first year in college was still active. He'd read *The Monkey Wrench Gang* and several other of Edward Abby's novels in high school. Seward might not have grown up in the Southwest, but the encroachment of man on nature was everywhere. The characters in Abby's novels took action. They didn't wait around for justice. They took revenge on the behalf of billions of voiceless species and ecosystems that were being poached, abused, and degraded. "Actually, I wrote the charter when I was fifteen." He grinned, looking a little embarrassed.

Seward's smile quickly tuned into a vicious snarl when he saw the markings on the map Inez had unfolded. "Tell me you didn't." He pointed at a red fist drawn in Mecosta County, MI.

"Don't you listen to the news?" Inez put her hand on her hips.

"I try not to."

"We'll you should." She looked around the shop. "No radio?"

"I'd be tempted to listen to Minnesota Public Radio." He had allowed her to shift the conversation again, but he'd not give up. "I'd be tempted to get involved. But, being involved got me nowhere and nothing." He waved his hand around the shop. "If you really want to change the world, stop talking about it and do something local. Raise awareness in your community. Not only does this shop keep kids off the street and out of trouble, but if you check the logs," he pointed to the wall left of the front door, "You can see the amount of carbon and CO_2 we've prevented."

Inez shook her head. "What happened to you? You're soft." Inez started to fold up the map. "Soft like everyone else."

"Soft?" His hands twitched and his eyes opened wide. For a moment, he felt young – that he had to prove himself to her. In his early days, he'd let others goad him into action, which had never ended well.

He relaxed his hands. He wouldn't take the bait. Perhaps, he'd tell her a few stories about the old days, but he'd choose when and what stories carefully. Shifting his weight, he said, "Yeah. I guess I'm soft." He patted his belly and smiled.

"I knew it. You've been lulled into believing that the small things can actually make a difference."

"They do matter."

"No. No, they don't." She waved around at the mess he called a shop. "How many of your customers ride for more than enjoyment? How many use bikes as their main mode of transportation?"

"A few." Then he admitted, "But I haven't converted as many as I'd hoped."

"See." She pointed like scolding mother. "C4 is the only answer – a wake up call that can't be ignored."

"Okay. I admit I miss the thrill of more aggressive actions."

"Like what?"

"Well, there was one time when Al and I poured sand into the gas tanks of a few loggers." He chuckled. "The set back was so costly that the subdevelopment project was put on hold indefinitely. We saved a small grove of dogwood trees."

"Wow! You must have been cute back in the day, playing at Lorax. Did you speak for the trees?"

Seward snorted. "So, what did the hard-boiled-eco princess do?"

"I think you know."

"You attacked the water bottling plant in Mecosta County." Seward shook his head thinking that she'd likely broken in and tampered with the equipment. The damage would be a temporary setback, costing hundreds of thousands in lost hours of productivity. This was also likely his fault. He had drawn up detailed plans that outlined three options for engagement. Option 1: disrupt shipping. Option 2: disrupt pumping. Option 3. demolition. Demolition was never a real option. He had made that clear in the charter. Options 1 and 2 would result in criminal misdemeanors, while Option 3 would almost always result in a felony conviction if caught. "Which of my plans did you carry out, option 1 or 2, or a little of both?"

Inez twisted the map in her hands. "I blew it up."

Five

Seward didn't say anything for a few minutes. Instead, he felt the need to bang on something. He walked around the counter to his workstation and picked up a bent wheel rim and a truing mallet. Seward took a couple of swings at the rim, thwacks and twangs rang though the otherwise silent shop.

In between his hammer swings, he could hear Inez trying to tell him something, but the ringing in his ears blocked everything out. Until he thought he had heard her say something about Al and a railroad. He let his shoulders sag, and he put the mallet away. "Come again?" Seward turned around. "What was that about Al?"

"He told me that you were part of a railroad."

Seward snorted.

"Can you...I don't know." If she had been blond, she would have flipped her hair off her shoulder and pouted. She wasn't. So she demanded, "Make me disappear?"

"Disappear? Disappear. Did you even bother to read my activism manifesto?" Seward raised his hand. "Don't. I know you didn't. Abby's characters might have cut and run, but I sided with Henry David Thoreau. Civil disobedience without a face is nothing more than a pointless criminal act."

"Thoreau never said that."

"You're right. He didn't, but I did." Seward pulled a small leather box out from under near the register. He opened it and paused. "If no one takes credit for an act of extreme activism, it becomes a random act of violence."

Inez shifted her weight from one foot to the other. "Is that why you stuck around and got arrested? I just thought you were sloppy."

"Sloppy?"

Inez took a couple of aggressive steps forward. "Yeah, sloppy."

"I took responsibility. Taking responsibility is not sloppy." Seward didn't back down. Instead, he let Inez invade his personal space. She was close enough that he could feel the heat from her body. "Thoreau spent time in jail for tax evasion. He stood up for what he believed in. He followed though."

"The laws are different now. The acts are different."

"I disagree."

"You can disagree all you want, but I'm not going to jail." Inez stepped back. She turned her back to Seward. "Al told me that you might not want to help me, so he gave me a few other names, but he said to try you first." Inez pulled out a wad of bills. "If you need money..."

"Put your money away."

"So you'll help?"

"Yeah, I'll help." Seward stared to line up index cards on the display case. "But not until you tell me more about Al."

Inez picked up one of the cards. "What are these?"

"The railroad."

"What do you want to know about Al?"

"How is he?"

"Not good. I had to get special permission to visit him in the hospital."

"Let me guess..."

"He has lung cancer, but he couldn't stop talking about the good old days."

"Well, they weren't so good."

"You should go see him. I could tell you where he's staying. I know that's not how it works, but you should go see him. He seemed lonely."

"We're all lonely, and you're right, it's not how it works." Seward took the card back and placed it on the counter. "Are you ready?"

"Yes."

"You're sure." Seward looked into her eyes and saw a fierce quality that he could admire. "You only get one chance at this. If you answer any of the questions incorrectly, or I feel that you'd put the railroad at risk, I'll stop immediately. You'll be on your own."

"I'm ready."

Seward flipped over the first card.

Six

It had been a long time since Seward had used the railroad cards. He read the question on the card to himself a couple of times. He felt the answers flood back. It had been a simpler time when he'd written a plan for smuggling eco-fugitives, but most of the rules still applied. He wondered if the next station was even intact. Susan could have moved. She might be more out of practice than he was, and she might turn Inez down. Any number of things could go wrong. However, Seward had built a fragile system for a reason. He didn't want anyone to get hurt. Still, he didn't believe in running anyway. The only way to draw attention to a cause was to be caught, go to trial, go to jail, and to serve time.

Seward had only built the railroad at Helen's request. Seward had loved her, and she had gone along with his crazy stunts because she'd loved him. They'd planed a life together, but he'd needed to prove his values to a bunch of freshmen. He had let himself be arrested, and well, that was that.

He put the card down. "Fuck the test. Just talk to me." He brushed the cards into a pile, straightened them by tapping them on the counter, and sealed them back in the leather box. The test seemed distant and unreal, a hippie's dream. He liked to think of himself as a businessman now, someone who thought through things with reason and logic and didn't act on his passions. "Why did you run?"

Inez looked around. "Can we sit?"

"Sure." Seward motioned for her to come around the counter. He had three barstools behind the counter. He got up on one. "I'm just so used to standing all day that I forget that I have these."

"I..." Inez paused while she moved a seat closer. "I...The bomb that I used should have only taken out the plant's pumps. No big deal right. But something happened, and it razed the building."

"Shit."

"I'll be charged and tried as a domestic terrorist, a.k.a, Timothy McVeigh and Terry Nichols. You know the Oklahoma City bombers who took out the Federal building."

"Sure, I could see the charges being steep, but you didn't kill anyone, did you?"

Inez sucked on her lower lip.

"Did you?"

"The bomb killed five people."

Seward's mouth hung open. He knew that sometimes people got hurt when activists went too far. He'd known the risks. It was why he'd always hit small operations at night because he'd known they wouldn't have a third shift.

Inez began to sob. Her body shook. Hugging herself tightly, rivers of dark mascara ran down the sides of her nose. She started to gasp as if hyperventilating.

Seward asked himself why evolution had hardwired him with a sympathy gene for desperate women that triggered an irrational savior complex. He counted all of the destruction he'd caused over the years, and somehow he'd managed to only ever cripple machines. Even though he was thinking that he should call the cops and turn her in – perhaps they'd finally stop watching him – his body was up and moving. He found himself hugging her tightly to him. "Don't worry." Seward murmured. "We'll get you safely away."

Seven

Seward held Inez until she had calmed down. When he finally let go, he told her that she needed to get some rest, and that there was a cot in the back room. And like anyone else trying to recover from shock, he found comfort in routine. He had opened the shop just in time for the morning meeting of The Greenway Coalition, a group of concerned bike enthusiasts that helped keep the city's longest stretch of bike path clean and safe. They also petitioned the city council on a regular basis and were responsible for the construction of a hundred new miles of converted railway and side-of-street bike paths.

The Greenway Coalition had made Seward's Custom Cycle Repair & Junk Yard one of their home bases. Seward was a member. The shop was only a block away from one of The Greenway's on-off ramps in the Uptown area. It was also located across the street from a couple of coffee joints and a hipster bowling ally and restaurant that was popular with the single-speed and fixed-gear crowds. The synergy of the neighborhood worked.

Seward noted that their ride was going to be light today. There were only three cyclists sifting through parts. When the ride was this light, he'd typically close the shop and join in. He had Inez to worry about, but he needed to clear his head, and he felt like a ride. He wrote a quick note for Inez and taped it where she would find it, on the handlebars of her Big Dummy.

"I'll ride along today."

Jason, a single-speed fanatic that rode a self-constructed grasshopper green road bike with white tires and handle grips said, "Great, we're really short today." He looked around the shop. "What are you going to take out?"

"My chopper." Seward pointed to a tomato red cruiser with tires that were big enough to support a small motorcycle. The frame was elongated and based on Kustom Kruisers' Sick Daddy, but with the modifications that Seward had added, it looked more like Tetsuo's low-rider motorcycle from the animated film *Akira*.

"Cool." Jason asked, "Do you think that you'll be able to keep up on that monster?"

"I just added new cruiser hubs that store some energy though friction, and then they release it when I stop pedaling.

They'll keep me going about twenty miles an hour, so the question is, can you keep up?"

"You're cheating. Where's the fun it that?"

"Hey, these babies will have more average people commuting to work on bikes this year and next. They're worth it." Seward pushed his bike to the door. "Besides not everyone can be as cool and hip as you."

"What do you mean by that?"

Then, the rider of an elite road bike, dressed in all the proper clothes piped in and said, "Jason, you're kind of an ass."

Eight

Seward fell in behind the others after they hit the Greenway. He might have talked up his riding skills, but he knew that he was a slower rider. They were going to average twelve to eighteen miles-per-hour, while he hung back between seven and ten. When he saw Jason look over his shoulder, Seward waved him on. He hadn't joined them on the ride to keep up; he had wanted some time away from Inez and the shop to think. Something about Inez didn't seem right and he couldn't put his finger on it yet.

For a few minutes, Seward just enjoyed the ride. The Greenway was busy this morning. There were families, in-line skaters, commuters, joggers, and walkers; name a mode of fossil-fuel-free transportation, and it could be found on the Greenway.

Seeing all those people using human power to move around gave Seward hope.

There was one couple on a tandem bike having difficulty deciding who was in charge. If they were smart about it, they would quickly determine that the person in front should make decisions about turning and speed. The trick to a two-person ride was communication. If they were going to turn, the lead position should find a way to signal the person in the back or they could topple. The same thing went for stopping and starting; it took coordination and practice, which this couple obviously didn't posses.

After Seward passed the couple on the tandem bike, he relaxed a little more and turned his thoughts to Inez. *Damn women,* he thought. *If a guy would have walked in and asked for the same kind of help, I would have told him to fuck off; but a dark haired woman is another story.*

Before he knew it, Seward was pulling to a stop at the Hiawatha Bike Trail Overpass, next to Jason and the others.

"Seward," Jason said, "We're going on to Minnehaha Falls before we turn around."

"Sure. I have to re-open the shop, so I'll catch up with you guys tomorrow morning."

"I knew you'd cut it short."

"I have a business to run."

"Sure. Excuses."

"Jason, you're an ass." Seward shifted his weight and started to back up.

"Whatever."

"Bye," Seward waved, and he sat on his chopper watching the others ride off for a few minutes before turning around to ride back to the shop.

The sun was still low in the sky, so as Seward rode west he decided to lose the sunglasses. As he approached the Bryant Ave exit ramp near his shop, his shoulders tightened up.

Inez.

On the ride back, he had committed to helping her, and when he was done, he had decided to go see Al in the hospital – rules or no rules. Still, he had a bad feeling that helping Inez was taking him down a path that he did want to go down, a path that he had thought he'd gotten off of years ago.

As he pulled out the keys to unlock the door to his shop, he noticed a white van parked on the eastbound side of West Lake Street. The logo on the side indicated a plumbing service that he'd never seen before today. However, he couldn't remember the last time he'd looked for a plumber.

Had this business with Inez made him jumpy, or was his paranoia of covert government operatives shifting in to a higher gear? Cautiously, Seward flipped the shop sign to OPEN and parked his chopper. Then, he Googled "Jed's Emergency Plumbing."

Nine

Seward's search results generated hundreds of entries for emergency plumbers, and only three for Jed's. Each of those entries was for speculative websites that claimed to monitor the movements of several Federal agencies. Before Seward panicked, he refined his search to include Minnesota. Again, his results only generated speculative websites. Now, Seward thought it was likely that his internet searches were being monitored, and whoever was in the van knew that he had discovered that Jed's Emergency Plumbing was a front.

Instead of panicking, which was what he really wanted to do right then, he pulled out a blank work order, and started making two lists: 1) Pros, 2) Cons, for helping Inez. It was soon obvious what his next course of action should require of him. He should walk outside, cross the street, and knock on the side of the van. He should give Inez up. His work in the community was worth more than the affections of a beautiful woman.

What the hell am I doing, Seward thought as he crumpled up the work order. *She needs my help*. If he'd allow himself a bit of honesty, he could have saved himself some time. He'd grown tired of the shop and the customers with their overly basic questions about brakes, flat tires, and derailed chains. He was ready for something else, preferably somewhere else too – somewhere warmer.

Seward walked back to the spare room. Before he knocked, his imagination got away from him. He saw her naked on a sandy beach somewhere south, but before he could fully explore the scenario, the door opened.

Inez stood in the doorway. She was wearing one of his blue work shirts. The shop's crank-and-gear logo rested above her left breast. She had left the top four buttons unfastened, and her tan legs were bare. She rubbed sleep from her eyes and ran her fingers through her hair.

Seeing Inez in one of his work shirts was better than anything he had started to imagine. Struggling to keep his composure, he asked, "Umm...yeah. Do you know by chance if you were followed?" He lifted his arm to point to the front of the store. "Because I'm fairly certain that the Feds are parked out front."

Inez's eyes popped open. She looked a like deer caught in headlights, panicked, defenseless, and unable to move. She managed to squeak out, "Help me."

Ten

"Put on some clothes." Seward turned back to the shop to let her get dressed, but spun around. "But keep the shop shirt on. Today, you're my newest hire. Oh, and you should find a cap back there too."

Seward was determined not to panic. He had been to prison once before. It was bad, but not movie bad. His rational mind was screaming at him to think things through and do the correct thing, but he wasn't thinking with his rational mind. Seward wanted to return to the road, picking up where he'd left off. Blowing up a water bottling plant was a gutsy move, one he had to admire. However, he had let that thought go as a couple of suits waked in the door.

Seward walked out from behind the counter, "Can I help you?" He pulled a yellow cloth out from his belt and cleaned his hands a bit before offering it to the gentlemen in black suits and glasses.

They shook hands.

"Agent Farth," he motioned to his partner, "And this is Agent Gaines."

While Agent Farth was tall and lean, Agent Gaines was short and stocky. They were the proverbial odd couple. Agent Gaines had an athletic build, a full head of hair, and a pleasant smile, while Agent Farth was lean, looked malnourished, and was bald.

"Are you in the market for a new bike?" Seward walked out from behind the counter and over to a row of mountain bikes, hybrids, and couple of single-speeds. "If I don't have what you're looking for today, I can order something, or I can put you on a watch list. I hit all the local auctions." Seward winked. "I've had good luck at the police auctions."

The agents looked at each other and shook their heads. Agent Gaines took off his sunglasses. His eyes were light blue rimmed in an amber circle of golden yellow, giving him a strange Siberian husky look.

"Have you been contacted by this woman?" Agent Gaines held out a picture of woman with long chestnut hair and pale skin. "Her name is Inez Wick."

Seward took the picture from Agent Gaines and stared at it for a few minutes. He was sure it was Inez, but damn. She didn't look anything like this photo now. "She's a looker. I'd remember her if she'd stopped in for anything."

Seward decided to push them. He wanted to know just how deep the shit ran. "Why do you think she'd stop here?"

Agent Farth answered, "She has connections to an activist group that you started at the University of Michigan." Agent Farth kept his cool, but he looked like he was holding back a caged tiger.

"You say activist like it's a dirty word or something." Seward took a step back. "But the only kind of activism I'm engaged in these days is organizing rides to keep The Greenway safe in the early morning and late evenings for bicycle commuters."

There was an awkward silence as Inez walked out from the backroom. She'd found a cap and wore it low. She was also carrying a couple of boxes new tubes. "You want me to put these on the shelves?"

"Yeah, but this time make sure that you watch the sizes. Some guy bought a sixteen inch when he needed a twenty-six inch."

Seward turned back to the agents. "I help out the community by taking in troubled teens and teaching them a skill they can use." Seward puffed up his chest a little and said, "Just last week I helped a young man, who didn't even have his G.E.D., get a paying job down the street fixing bikes for The Alt."

Agent Gaines suddenly looked tired. His smile drooped, and lines appeared in his forehead and around his eyes. "If she does stop by, please let us know." He held out his card.

Seward took the card. "Homeland Security?"

Agent Farth took a few quick steps forward so that he was almost touching Seward's chest with his own. "If Homeland Security would have existed while you and your…" He paused and broke a toothy grin. "We would have rounded up your domestic terrorist cell, I mean *activists*, and that would have been that."

"Farth!" Agent Gaines commanded. "We're leaving." Agent Gaines then turned to look at Seward one last time before putting his sunglasses back on, "We are watching you. We have good intelligence that suggests that Inez Wick will try to make contact."

Seward held Agent Gaines' card with both hands as he watched them exit and close the shop door behind them.

Eleven

Seward took a long deep breath in through his nose, and pushed out his upper lip so that the gray whiskers in his mustache tickled the tip of his nose. It wasn't a good look. He looked as if he'd just smelled something foul or tasted something bitter. Either way, it made him look more his age.

Seward got out his wallet, a floppy thing he'd hand stitched out of a used bike inner tube, and he flopped it open. Besides a few singles, his wallet contained his debit card and credit card, his driver's license, and his expired memberships to The Sierra Club, Green Peace, and EarthFirst! He slid Agent Gaines' card in over his driver's license.

"How can I thank you?" Inez had stopped working and turned around. She had chain grease on her arm and was holding a 3/8" wrench. She'd still left too many buttons unfastened, and she was smiling.

Seward had a couple inappropriate thoughts, but he remembered that she was young enough to be his daughter, so instead he said, "You can finish tuning up that rock-jumper and watch the store. I've got to make a couple of calls." Without saying anything else or holding eye contact, he made his way though the hall and out the back door.

He pulled his cell out of his pocket and looked up a number of an old friend, and he was about to press the number when he remembered that the agents were still parked out front. He reasoned that they had likely found his cell phone number already and tapped it, so his phone was useless. He looked around the alley behind his shop. It didn't look like anyone was watching, so he put his phone away and waked the two blocks through the back alleyway to Verizon.

As soon as he walked in, he was accosted by an over-caffeinated salesman who smelled like he bathed in spice and lavender.

The salesman said, "Welcome to Verizon Wireless. Can I help you?"

"Yes." Seward wasted no time. "I need a prepay. I'm thinking a thousand minutes."

"Sir," the salesman took a step back and turned up his nose. "We don't sell prepays. Try across the street at CVS." And without missing a beat, he moved past Seward to greet a woman in heels carrying a small, tired looking dog under her arm. "Welcome to Version. Can I help you?"

Seward shook his head. *Okay*, he thought, *CVS*.

After selecting a bar-phone that looked like it was at least ten years old, Seward sat on the curb outside CVS. He found his friend's number on his cell and called it on the prepay. After a few rings, Seward's call went to voice mail.

"Cooper, it's Seward. I'm using a prepay. Don't call me on a line in your name." Seward left his prepay's number and got up. He walked back across Lake Street and down Dupont Avenue to the alleyway and headed back to his shop.

Okay, Seward thought, *I made the call.*

Twelve

Back in the shop, Inez was still busy, playing the dutiful clerk. It looked like she was done with the bike, and she was now cleaning and detailing it. It was warm in the shop, and Inez had rolled up her sleeves and fanned herself with an old newspaper with greasy chain marks all over it.

Fine job, Seward thought as he watched her pull the bike down off the stand. *If only she were a few years older and not in so fucking deep*. He left that thought unfinished and chastised himself, he wasn't that old yet, and if she made the first move, they were both consenting adults. Who was he to place limits on these things?

"I made a call."

Inez looked up from her work. "I could almost forget why I was here." She wiped her forehead with the back of her arm exposing yet another tattoo on the underside of bicep near her armpit: green lettering, which said, 'All Natural Woman.' "I can see why you like this work."

Seward puzzled over this tattoo for a second. She had shaved pits, legs, and sculpted eyebrows, which made the tattoo seem out of place. Seward let it go with a sigh. Who was he to make assumptions about what an 'All Natural Woman' should look like? Just because the women he'd known who'd used that slogan didn't shave, trim, or wax anything in his day, didn't mean a new generation couldn't adopt and redefine the slogan. Seward compared her tattoo to the movement he'd tried to start, and he could see that Inez's generation had kept what they liked and discarded what they didn't. A Bob Dylan song popped into Seward's head that colored the room and his opinion of Inez in a deep shade of amber, which Seward thought to be lovely and made Inez that much more beautiful.

"It looks like the work suits you." *Lame*, Seward thought, *very lame*. "I'm waiting for a phone call, but here's what I need you to do." Seward fell in to his role of helpful store manager who shows at-risk youth around the store, giving directions and orders. Giving directions calmed his nerves a little and allowed him to see Inez as labor instead of as a sexy tree-hugging damsel in distress. He told himself that was where their relationship needed to start and end: he was in charge and she would do what he said.

Within a few minutes, Seward's van was loaded with several bikes that he needed to deliver today, along with Inez's Big Dummy and the rest of her things. He'd tossed his Long Hall, along with some gear, into the van. Once a month, Seward would take a group of local Scouts on a bike-and-camp trip that started at the shop ended just north of Maple Grove. The ride took about six hours one way with some of the younger Scouts in tow, but everyone had a good time, and no one complained or asked "Are we there yet?" so Seward thought the experience blissful.

"Where are we going with all of these bikes?"

"We're going to deliver them."

"But I thought..."

Seward's prepay phone rang twice. Seward held up his hand and walked a short distance down the alley before answering.

Thirteen

"Dan, its Cooper."

"I have a bike that needs to be delivered in the next couple of days. Do you think that you can help?"

"Destination?"

"Out of country. I was thinking somewhere south." Seward sucked in and bit his lower lip. He hadn't spoken with Cooper in years. Their last interaction had been cold, frigid really, and they had agreed to have nothing to do with each other ever again. However, by the way Cooper was going about business on the phone, Seward's hopes were high that they would be able to workout their differences.

"Fanny Jones just went south. Chile, I think."

"That'll work."

"Can you get the bike down river, or you need me to pick it up?"

Seward looked at Inez sitting in the open side door of his delivery van. He hadn't thought about passing Inez off to another in the railroad. Passing her off was the next logical step, which is how the railroad was supposed to work and keep the spooks guessing. However, he'd already forgone the test, and he'd already interacted with two federal agents. It seemed he was committed to another adventure. He knew it would be his last real chance to take part in something more subversive than the annual May Day Parade and festival.

Seward puffed up his chest and said, "No, I'll deliver."

"How far?"

"The whole way."

"Wow, man. She must be a pretty special bike."

"She is."

"You ride her yet?"

"No."

"Is there hope?"

Seward felt his jeans tighten. A little embarrassed, Seward turned away from Inez and the delivery van. "Look, can you help?"

"Sorry, man. I didn't mean anything by it."

"What do you need from me?"

"I need pictures. On your way down, you'll need to stop at, I don't know, somewhere you can get headshots, like a Kinko's."

"That it?"

"Yeah, that'll do it."

"Cooper, just to warn you, this bike is hot, so if you want out, I'll understand. I don't want another misunderstanding between us."

"Shit man, is that why we haven't… Well, I guess I could have called you too. What happened in Albuquerque is history, man."

Seward let his shoulders slump and he leaned against the building. "Here I thought you still blamed me for Julie."

"No, man. Listen. Julie was wildfire. It was only a matter of time before something happened to her. I'm just glad that we didn't go down with her."

"Okay, I have a few local deliveries before I can skip town. Will two days give you enough time?"

"Sure enough."

"Okay. Two days."

"Two days."

Seward waited for Cooper to hang up, but he didn't hear the line disconnect and the phone wasn't giving him disconnected static. It was beeping as if there'd been a third party listening in. Seward wanted to chalk the strange silence up to a cheap phone, but he knew better. He knew that his prepay was too new to have a bug, but he wasn't so sure about Cooper's phone.

Seward pulled himself off the wall and walked over to the delivery van. He looked down at Inez, and he asked, "You ready to go?"

Fourteen

Inez sat in the back of the van with the bikes. She had turned over a yellow milk crate and was using it as a seat. She leaned with the van as it turned corners and slid a little when the van came to a stop at traffic signals. "How much does delivery cost?"

"Gas, miles, and tip."

"How many bikes do you deliver?"

"Not many. Most of my customers live around the area, just a few blocks from the shop, but I do get a few folks from as far away as Burnsville and Maple Grove."

"How far's that?"

"15 to 20 minutes."

Inez looked at the tag hanging off an expensive looking road bike. "If you can afford a Delta 7 Ascend, why bring it to your shop?" Inez dropped the tag. "I mean…I don't mean to…"

"No worries. You don't know me, and I guess what you do know of me is practically ancient history." Seward tried to adjust his rearview mirror so that he could see Inez in the back, but he couldn't find the right angle. "There are very few people in the United States that can be trusted to work on a D7A, and I guess I'm one of them, or I guess I should say, I was one of them."

"What do you mean, *was?*" Inez shifted on her box.

"I don't think anyone followed us. You can come up front." Seward looked over the back of his seat. "We're far enough south now."

As Inez crawled into the passenger's seat, she asked, "Where are we going? I thought that St. Louis Park was only a few minutes away."

"We're about a half-hour south on HWY 35." Seward looked over at Inez. He thought she looked innocent, or was it her question that made her seem that way? "The D7A and the others back there," Seward hitched his thumb over his shoulder, "represent your train ticket."

Inez buckled her belt and put her feet on the dash. "But those bikes aren't yours."

"Oh, so now the hardened eco-terrorist is worried about the theft of a couple of road bikes," Seward laughed.

"A couple of road bikes," Inez sat up. "The D7A's frameset goes for what, 6K, and it looks like it has all the trim, so it must be worth at least 15K or 16K."

"I'm impressed. You know your bikes." Seward pulled out a map and tossed it into Inez's lap. "Open that. Oh, and if you're still wondering, there's roughly 200K in the back, and I think that's just in the bikes that are built up."

While Inez unfolded the map, she said, "If I had a D7A, I'd lojack it."

"Well, actually the Delta 7 Ascend is traceable, but I know where the GPS chip is located, and I'll take care of it soon. The owner won't think to look for it for a few days. He is, well, I guess now, *was* a good friend." Seward shook his head. He was starting truly to buy into Inez's innocence. He could see that she had no idea that in order to help her, he'd given up the shop. He was now on the run, too.

Inez finished unfolding the map. "Okay, so now what?"

"So what do you think?"

"It looks like a map of Chile."

Seward waited. He knew it would sink in, but she was taking her sweet time realizing just what running meant for her life. He wasn't going to tell her the specifics just yet. In time, he might tell her his plan to meet Cooper in Louisiana, pick up forged documents, and take a pleasure cruise down and around the tip of South America before beginning a new life in exile. He knew that his bike repair skills would help him find work in Chile. Parts of The country were used as an Olympic training ground for both winter and summer athletes, because of its varied climates and altitudes. Seward knew he'd come out on top, but he was beginning to worry about Inez.

"I don't understand." Inez turned the map over and over before folding it up again. "Why do we need a map of Chile?"

"Verá. Verá." *You'll see*, he thought.

Fifteen

Inez shifted several times, crossing and uncrossing her legs. She pushed herself upright in her seat, and then she slouched.

"Are you okay over there?" Seward asked.

"Could you pull over somewhere, so that I can use a bathroom?"

"Emergency?" Seward scanned the road a head. He spotted a road sign. "Can you wait a few minutes? There's a gas station a few miles up the road, or do you need me to pull over here?"

"I can wait."

"You sure?" Seward hiked his thumb over his shoulder. "Now that I think of it, there must be a couple of empty containers in the back somewhere. We can dump it out when we stop."

"I can wait. Can we talk about something else or listen to the radio?"

"The radio is busted. I don't usually take the van on long trips."

"Don't you think that the guys out front will have noticed that we're not coming back?" Inez crossed her legs again and sucked on her lower lip.

"Yeah, they'll notice."

"Won't they start looking for your van?" Inez spread her arms as if she were Vanna White turning letters on Wheel-of-Fortune. "I mean it has a picture of your face on the side of it."

"What?"

"I'm just saying."

"Okay. I'll take care of it when we stop." Seward pointed at the side of the road. "Here we go."

Seward exited HWY 35, and he pulled in beside a gas pump at a BP station. Inez had jumped out, and she had run for the convenience store before he had even had the chance to turn the van off and put it into park. Seward got out and filled the tank. Then he walked around his van. He loved the picture of him on his chopper. A friend had taken it as a joke, but Seward loved it, so he had it made into a large magnet.

Carefully, trying not to damage the magnet, he peeled it off the side. It was flexible enough to loosely roll up, but he didn't have a tube or anything to tie it with, so he went into the store with the intention of buying rope.

He walked up and down the isles looking at all the different types of chocolate bars, gum, and bags of sweet and salty things before making his way to the automotive section where he picked up some rope. As he was paying for the rope and gas, he looked up into the security mirror above the clerk. In the mirror, he could see Inez. She was talking adamantly on one of the pay phones. Her body language, the flailing of arms, the set of her hips, and how she white knuckled the receiver, told Seward she was upset. However, she didn't look upset in the way he expected. It looked more as if she was giving instructions to a child who didn't listen the first three times to clean his room.

Seward finished up at the register, and he went back out to his van and stored the magnet in the back with the bikes. He got in and waited. As he sat there, he started to have doubts about Inez again. She had just shown up out of nowhere, and here he was helping her. What did he know about her other than what she had told him? As far as he knew, she could have been on the phone with the Feds. This whole scenario could have been constructed to ensnare him, his contacts, and his friends. She was in the store, on the phone, right now, reporting their location and asking for help, back up because no one expected a middle-aged, has-been eco-activist to take off with a young girl in order to fulfill some wet dream he had had as an undergrad in college.

Seward looked in the driver's side mirror. He could feel the open road calling him back. He looked into the rearview and saw the darkness envelop bikes and bike parts. He then twisted the rearview and looked into his own eyes. He thought, *Seward has had a good run. It might be time for a change.* In that moment, his soft friendly eyes wrinkled and hardened.

The passenger door opened. "I see that you've taken the ad down."

Seward took along deep breath before turning to look at Inez. "Who were you talking to on the phone?"

Sixteen

"Phone?" Inez buckled the seatbelt. The delivery van was so old it didn't have a cross-strap. Each time Inez buckled-up, she looked a little confused at its absence. After fumbling with the buckle, she looked straight ahead repositioning her bare feet on the dash.

Seward started the van and pulled away. He'd press her again in a few minutes, when they were on the highway. For some reason, Seward found that people were honest at high speeds. However, he was impatient. So, as he pulled on the on-ramp, he asked again.

Inez didn't budge.

To Seward, she looked like she was trying to pretend to fall asleep. *What was it with women*, Seward thought, *that they could so easily devolve from perky-go-lucky to bitchy-go-cranky?* Either way, she was going to have to tell him something. Whatever she told him, he'd decided that it would likely be a lie.

Shifting her weight a little, Inez asked, "When did you get your scar?"

"Scar?" He knew exactly what she was asking about, but he wanted her to be specific. He needed her to engage him in conversation, so he could read her responses. He was good at lie detecting. He had known she hadn't been forthright with him from the start, but he hadn't had this much fun in years. *Fun*, he thought, *it all really comes down to fun. Am I so simple?*

"The one behind your right ear that curves down your neck, how far does it extend?" She sat up, removing her feet from the dash.

"Her name was Julie Ryerson. She died in Albuquerque." He paused to focus on the road. An eighteen-wheeler passed on the left disrupting the headwind just enough that he had to compensate to keep the van on the road. After it passed, Seward was able to pick up where he left the story.

"Julie was lovely. The kind of firecracker that could ignite the soul of the most calloused man." Seward looked over at Inez, taking his eyes off the road to meet hers. "She was a lot like you." He quickly resumed watching the road.

"Julie died for the cause. She was leading a protest of eighty concerned environmentalists who were trying to have a specific species of butterfly added to the endangered species list. The locals were not amused."

"Why?" Inez asked, "Wouldn't the preservation of a species help to create an eco-tourist destination?"

"Yes. It would have, but the habitat in which the species resided had already been turned into a series of mixed-use nature trails. The most profitable type of tourism was from off road bikes. The town hosted several motocross competitions every year, including the X-Games."

"So, couldn't a compromise work?"

"Compromise! *Compromise*, are you for real?" Seward had to ease up off the gas. He noticed that he was pushing his van a little too hard. "You just blew up a water bottling plant, and you want to talk about compromise?"

"Hey. I tried to compromise with them." Inez was leaning forward in her seat one hand on the dash. "I had asked them to slow down, pump a little slower and allow more water from the spring to travel down river."

"So you know how it is."

"Yes, I fucking do."

"Good. Now you know how Julie felt when the town wouldn't budge. They didn't want to see their tourism dry up just because some butterflies' habitat needed to be protected. They saw their livelihoods in jeopardy."

"What do you mean?"

"About what?"

"The stuff about protecting habitat jeopardizes livelihoods."

Seward had her. He would now have to double check everything she had told him. She was no environmentalist, and she hadn't taken classes from the University of Michigan in any scientific field. If she had, she'd have known the answer to her own question.

"Okay. Let me put it this way: The EPA, under the second Bush administration – that's Bush Jr. – proposed adding the Polar Bear to the endangered species list even though the species' numbers didn't qualify its addition." Seward let out a long sigh. "These are the issues that get my blood fired up, sorry. Anyway, the proposal was denied. Any guesses why?"

"No." Inez shrugged her shoulders. "You just said there were plenty of them running around."

"True. However, the proposal predicted that the Polar Bear's numbers would drop significantly in just a few years because their habitat was fragmenting too quickly for the species to adapt."

"Do you know what happens when a species is added to the endangered species list?" Seward asked.

"Sure. We protect it."

"Yes, we do protect it, but when a species is added to the endangered species list, we go further – we attempt to help it recover."

Inez butted in, "How?"

"We have to protect the species' habitat. The only way to ensure the protection of a species is to protect its habitat."

"So we protect its habitat. What's the big deal?"

"Where do Polar Bears live?"

"The North Pole."

"Correct. So?"

Inez was slow to answer, "We'd have to protect the North Pole."

"Yes, which would mean we'd have to find a way to slow the retraction of polar sea ice, which, in turn, would mean we would have to do something about anthropomorphic climate change."

"I thought we were talking about Polar Bears?" Inez asked.

"We are. In order to protect the Polar Bear, we would need to solve climate change, because climate change is fragmenting the Polar Bear's habitat, and we can't help the Polar Bear if we can't preserve its habitat – its ecosystem."

Confused, Inez asked, "Weren't we talking about Julie and your scar?"

"No." Seward said, sternly. "I wanted to know who you were yelling at on the phone back at the gas station."

Seventeen

Seward pulled the van over onto the side of the road. Without looking at Inez, he turned off the van's engine. From under this seat, he pulled a gun and pointed it at Inez's chest. The gun was small, sliver, and loaded. To prove that he was serious, he pointed the gun at the roof and fired. The small gun snapped like a cap gun the kids in the neighborhood played with on summer afternoons. Unlike the plastic replicas, his gun put a small hole in the roof.

Pointing the gun back at Inez's chest, "I'm only going to ask each question once." He was calm. He'd been in situations like this one before. Still, his outstretched arm with the gun quivered slightly. Smiling, he relaxed further by lowering the gun, but he kept it aimed, his finger on the trigger.

Inez sat very still. Her hands were open and rested on her lap. "If you look in my bag, you'll find your answers."

At hearing her confession, Seward didn't hesitate. He fired a killing shot.

Eighteen

Seward replaced the small gun under his seat. Before moving, he watched traffic on 35 slide by his van. He took a couple of deep breaths and steadied himself. He asked the silence, "How many people have I killed over the years? How many people have I had to become?"

No answer.

He got out of the van. He needed to work quickly. No telling how long before someone would pull over to help or worse. Highway Patrol would be by soon, and he didn't want to be on the side of the road.

Opening the passenger door, the pool of blood that had accumulated dripped on to the asphalt. Seward pulled Inez out and dumped her body over the highway embankment. Inez's body rolled slowly and came to a halt at the bottom.

Seward pulled cleaning equipment out of the back and started to scrub the passenger's seat. The blood wasn't easy to sop up, but he made short work of the seat and floor mat. *What a waste*, he thought. Inez had been a pretty girl. He'd hoped that she was legit. The reservations he'd made for exiting the US were real, and now he'd exit alone.

Back in the driver's seat, he started the van. He pulled out from the shoulder and made his way to the next major highway. He could have taken 35 most of the way, but that wouldn't have been smart. Instead, he chose to take 90 West, knowing that he'd have to double back eventually.

While he drove, he pulled an envelope from under the dash near the steering column. Opening it, he dumped a pile of passports onto his lap. "I'm not going back to prison. I'm not going back." He picked one: Rupert Earlson, Henderson, MN. He thought about Rupert for a while. What types of things did Rupert like? What did Mr. Earlson do for a living?

One thing was for sure, Rupert Earlson wasn't a bike mechanic. He needed to unload the bikes and trade in his van for something sportier. Rupert was a poor teacher of English that wanted to see the world before he died of AIDS/HIV. In order to make his dreams of seeing the world come true, he'd signed on to teach in foreign countries. His first stop was Peru, but he planned to hit Korea, China, and Japan.

Before Seward could become Rupert Earlson, he'd need to clean up a few loose ends that Daniel Emmett Seward had created. As much as he cared about his bike shop and the community that he'd lived in for the last several years, it was his connection to Al that gave him the most reason to pause. The only way that the Feds could have found him was to go through Al. Al was the only person who knew his true identity. Before he could become the traveling English teacher, he'd have to take care of Al.

Seward new that if what Inez had told him about Al was true, and he believed her, he'd find him in a hospital. Al was a sickly fellow and if anyone was going to die of cancer at an early age, it was going to be him. Seward pounded his hands on the steering wheel. Al was the only one who knew all of his aliases. Seward would just have to hope that on his deathbed, Al had forgotten a couple of them.

"Ah! The life of an eco-terrorist," Seward said over the hum of his van. "You blow a couple of buildings up and kill a few people, and the government won't rest until you're behind bars or dead. However, if you're a multi-billion dollar industry that pollutes the air and the water, killing thousands, the government gives you a tax break for creating jobs." Frustrated, he punched the van's steering wheel three times. On the third, he accidently sounded the van's horn.

What made him truly angry wasn't having to kill Inez, but was that he'd changed personas so many times since leaving prison that he didn't remember his real name. Up until this moment, he had been Daniel Emmett Seward and had been his entire life. His immersion into Seward's life had been so perfect that he had started to even fool himself, but killing Inez – that brought back memories.

Nineteen

He sat next to Al's bed in the cancer wing of the Mayo Clinic in Rochester, MN. He had spent the last few weeks unloading the bikes that he'd stolen from his shop's customers though Craigslist. It'd taken time. People were skeptical of sellers with quality merchandise. However, he had perfected the listing ratio for quality goods long ago: too high a price, no sale; too low, buyers were scared off because they'd think that the items were hot. While he waited for responders to his bike ads, he'd watched for news articles about Inez or a dead Fed, but not a single one surfaced, which further confirmed the danger he had been in trying to help her. He hadn't had the heart to look in her bag. Instead, he'd dumped it further along the Highway. He'd also had time to search for Al and perfect his new persona.

Al wasn't difficult to run down. Al hadn't gone to prison and wasn't seen as a risk to society. The only part Al had played was information keeper for their eco-club. When he let himself think about the old days when he and Julie had been extremists, he'd thought a lot about Al. He wondered if Al had been the one to leak the information the Feds had used to land him in prison.

He could talk the talk. In fact, the man who went by the name Daniel Emmett Seward believed all the ethical, civil disobedience horseshit that he'd fed the kids who'd worked in his shop over the years. He thought that if he could have remained Daniel Emmett Seward for a few more years, he would have come to believe it too.

Sitting next to Al's bed felt pathetic. He knew that even if Al woke up and saw him sitting next to the bed that Al wouldn't recognize him. In his search for Al, he had transformed himself into Rupert Earlson. While Daniel Emmett Seward had a beer gut, wore glasses, and had hippie-chic brown hair, Rupert Earlson had foppish blond-red hair, was anorexic and walked with a limp. Rupert Earlson was also awkwardly tan. He had gone to a couple of tanning beds and sunk in his shorts and a t-shirt with too long short sleeves that covered his elbows. However, when Rupert Earlson walked around town, he wore Khaki shorts with a belt and an ill-fitting button-down short sleeved shirt with a black tie. His look attracted a lot of attention, which he liked. He thought of it as hiding in the open. People would look at him once and dismiss him.

He stood up and took the two steps needed to cross over to Al's bed. He pulled the pillow out from under Al's head and pressed it over Al's mouth. In Al's already weak condition, he died quickly, without a fight. Leaving the pillow on top of Al's face, The man who had been Seward and who was now Earlson walked out of the room.

Twenty

In the small village of Iio, Peru, at the corner of San Pedro and Elias Aguirre, Rupert Earlson stood at the front of a classroom. He wrote down the parts of basic speech: Noun, Verb, Pronoun, Adjective, Adverb, Preposition, Conjunction, Interjection. He lectured for a few minutes, giving examples of each. Then he grouped his students into five groups, giving each a piece of chalk.

"Pick someone to write on the board for your group." Earlson moved to the back of the class while his students picked a writer. After a few minutes, each group had one person standing at the board. Earlson called out, "Adverb."

The students sitting in their seats shouted and cheered, while the writers raced to write as many adverbs on the board as they could chalk in the two minutes Earlson had given them. It was a fun game. However, the parts of speech were not fun or easy to learn, but games bought out the competitive side in the students.

After a few rounds, the students were still excited. The writers at the board knew that injections had to be next. It was the only part of speech left, and it was the most fun because it included swears and curses followed by an exclamation point.

Earlson smiled for the first time in weeks. As he said, "Interjection," he started his stopwatch, he saw two men in dark suits and sunglasses standing in the doorway. Earlson's smiled sagged. He thought, *Just two more weeks and I'd have been ready to take out the timber mill.* The mill was illegally logging and selling the timber back to the people of Iio.

"Stop!" Earlson yelled. He walked up to the board. He erased misspelled worlds and words that weren't interjections. When he was done awarding points, the wining team cheered as if they were at a fútbol match. After the class settled down, he dismissed them.

Earlson erased the board and banged the erasers before walking over to greet his guests. "What can I do for you?"

Agent Gaines asked, "Rupert Earlson?"

"Yes." Earlson limped over to a chair. He sat down and pointed the agents to the classroom desks. "I am he."

"We believe that you might be able to help us locate someone," said Agent Farth. "Do you have a few minutes to answer a couple of questions?"

"Sure."

"Has a Daniel Seward contacted you?"

"No. Should I be expecting him?"

"We believe that he might," Agent Farth held out his card, "come looking for you."

"Why?" Earlson took it and placed between the pages of his textbook. "I haven't seen him since college."

Agent Gaines said, "Just a hunch. You both attended the University of Michigan around the same time." He tried to get comfortable in the school desk then decided to stand. "You both were members of an environmentalist group that we've linked to several disturbances over the years."

Earlson stood. "Do you suspect me?" He put his hands over his mouth. "I only joined because there was this girl I liked."

Agent Farth stood and put a hand on Earlson's shoulder. "No. No. We're just following up on a few leads." He turned to Agent Gaines.

"However," Agent Gaines said, "Many of the club's members have been turning up dead, so we're here to warn you."

"Warn me? Should I be afraid?"

"We don't think so." Said Agent Gaines, "But then again, perhaps."

"What should I do?"

"If Daniel Seward contacts you, please call us." And with that, both agents shook Earlson's hand.

Earlson stood. "Well, thanks. I guess." His left shoulder slouched lower than this right.

As Agent Farth walked through the door, he said, "Nice gig you have here."

Twenty-One

Earlson made his way home to the three-person villa overlooking the Pacific Ocean atop a rocky cliff. His unit was the only one currently rented, and he preferred it that way. He couldn't afford the place on his own or he would have rented the entire building. The proprietor actively showed the other two rooms without success. It wasn't that the building was in disrepair that seemed to turn people away, but the lack of electricity.

It was late, but sunlight still trickled in the east facing windows over the ocean. Earlson made a habit of sitting on the west section of the wraparound deck each night. He enjoyed watching the setting sun turn orange and slip over the horizon. The way the sun disappeared, here one moment, gone the next as if it were a ball rolling off a table, confirming for Earlson that his world was flat. He knew that the globe was spherical but that didn't change his worldview: humans were opportunistic creatures just like every other species. Resources within reach were taken and horded to ensure personal genetic survival, despite the capacity for higher reasoning. It took an especially developed mind to appreciate the needs of others and act selfishly, so too it took an especially attuned person to see the connections that compose the biosphere.

As Earlson lit a candle and made his way to the outhouse, several yards from the main building, a few lines from *The Lorax* by Dr. Seuss ran though his head. Opening the door to the outhouse, he said aloud, "I speak for the trees."

The candle Earlson held out illuminated and cast long flickering shadows inside the outhouse. Bound and gagged, under the roll of toilet paper, a man who was Earlson's twin in appearance opened bruised eyes.

After setting the candle down, Earlson sat and retrieved a small notebook from the floor. He turned to his bound twin and asked, "Ready to continue?"

The bound twin nodded.

Earlson quickly removed the duct tape from his twin's mouth.

The twin whimpered, spit out a sock, and took a deep breath. "I need my medication."

Earlson produced a canteen of water, a small sandwich, and several large pills. "Here. Eat first." He held the sandwich up to his twin's mouth.

The twin took a bit and chewed. He then took water. "My pills."

Earlson put a couple in his twin's mouth and tipped the canteen. After feeding and medicating his twin, Earlson said, "Looks like we left off at your junior prom." He tapped a pen against his teeth. "You took a Heather Sloan, red hair, blue-green eyes. She wouldn't let you touch her."

A few minutes passed in silence.

Earlson rocked his twin with his foot, pen at the ready. "What happened next?"

Lady Aqua

One

Inez Wick set the last charge. Her gloved fingers pressed the buttons on the red plastic stopwatch. The green numbers started counting down from forty minutes, plenty of time to get out. Ten minutes had passed between setting each of the other two charges around the main pump. She'd set the first one for sixty and the second for fifty. With a little luck, they should detonate within seconds of each other.

She hadn't had the time or the money to get fancy with this job. She preferred military grade plastique and digital synchronized switches. She would have liked longer to plan the job, but she'd let her righteous anger overpower her judgment, which was a habit she knew she needed to kick. However, she'd felt that if she let go of her anger, her motivation would have followed. Someone had to fight back, someone had to take a stand, and that someone, she'd thought, needed to be a little crazy.

Escaping the building was going to be easy. Wearing company overalls, cap, and nametag, she stopped at the front desk.

"See you tomorrow night," she said, as she signed out using the name on her badge, Jennifer McInnis. "You're locking up soon, I hope."

The guard at the front desk was young. He had the distracted look of his generation. What should he check next: email, Facebook, Twitter, or email again? He barely managed to look up from his phone to say, "What?"

"You're going home soon?"

He looked at the clock. "Yeah. One last round and I'm out."

She looked at the clock and estimated that he'd be just starting his car when the charges detonated leveling the pump room. She didn't see the point in taking human life. Humans, just like every other species on the planet, were opportunistic creatures competing for resources. She only hoped that a little Monkey Wrench Gang-styled activism would call attention to her cause – wake people up a little.

However, unlike the characters in Abbey's novels, Inez didn't feel the need to stick around and watch. She was content to read newspapers and blogs. She did leave a calling card at each of her wake-up attempts, literally a business card with her adopted logo: a Tree of Life grasped tightly in a vertical fist. The image was an adaptation of the EarthFirst! fist logo.

She'd been a member of EarthFirst!, but found their methods of protest, lobbying and fundraising ineffective. She needed action, so she sought other models of action and found guidance in Abbey's gruff character, Hayduke. She didn't enjoy Abbey's fiction all that much, so she'd read only enough to be inspired. If Abbey's characters could figure out a way to blow up a newly constructed damn, she could do the same. She'd only needed to take a couple basic chemistry courses at the University of Michigan and make a couple of connections with a radical but under motivated environmental student organization on campus.

"Well, you better make it quick," she said.

"Sure. Sure." He was already back to thumbing his phone.

"Bye."

"Yeah."

Inez walked through the front door into the late evening. The stars were bright. She took a moment and located a few of her favorite constellations. Seeing the Three Sisters and Orion calmed her nerves. At this point in any job, she started to feel guilty. The destruction that would follow would only be a minor setback to production. She could only hope that by disrupting the pump, the river would again flow, restoring the mudflats downstream long enough to remind people of what they'd lost by allowing the water-bottling facility to be built at the river's source.

The North Star twinkled, and Inez shook her head. She had to leave. She shouldn't be around when the explosion tore down half the building. If she was going to make it downstream to where she planned to wait, she'd have to hurry now. She'd wasted too much time talking to the security guard and stargazing.

She found her car in the lot. At first, she didn't recognize it. She had put on false license plates and temporarily painted it a dark shade of blue. She walked past it and had to double back. Sloppy, she thought. What was her problem tonight? Usually, she was all business: in, out, done. Something just didn't feel right. Why were there still so many cars still in the lot?

She'd done the surveillance. Every night, the only car in the lot was the night guard. The night guard left every night at eleven-thirty. It was eleven-thirty now. The lot still had more than a dozen cars, including the night guard's. Something was wrong.

Inez ran back into the plant.

"Hey. What's going on tonight?" She was out of breath and panting. "Why are there still so many cars in the lot?"

Without looking up from his phone, "Pump three needed some maintenance."

"What?"

He put down his phone on the desk and looked at the security monitors. He motioned for her to come around the desk. He simply pointed.

"How long are you here tonight?"

"Until they're done." He picked up op the radio. "Security to work crew, ETA, over."

A few seconds pasted. "James, you got a hot date or something? You better call her. We're going to be all night."

He put the radio down and picked up his phone.

Inez's mind raced. If they were still down there when the charges detonated, they'd likely not die from the explosion but drown. She didn't have time to disconnect the charges.

"You okay?"

"I…"

"The restrooms are right over there." He pointed.

"There is a bomb in the main pump room." She reached over the counter and grabbed hold of the radio. She clicked it on, "Get out. Get out. There is a bomb in main pump room. You've got…" she looked at her watch. "…ten minutes."

She threw the radio at the guard and ran for the front door.

Two

Inez had scoured the news the next morning. She hadn't slept. Her thoughts continued racing even after a long hot bath. Ten minutes surely would have been enough time for the crew to get free of the pump room.

Too wound up to sleep, she'd turned on the TV to CNN, the radio to NPR, and live streamed news feeds on the computer. She was convinced the destruction of the water plant's pump room would receive national attention. She was also convinced she'd see her face and hear her name, since she'd taken the time to warn the repair crew, revealing that she knew about the bomb.

While the constant chatter of the news filled her tiny college dorm room, she packed. She wasn't going to stick around, get caught, and end up in prison or worse. Where did they send domestic eco-terrorists? She didn't want to find out what they'd do with her, so she'd take off on her bike, change her look, and seek out help where she could find it. She'd felt a little like Batman, except Batman didn't blow up industry. He usually, now that she thought about it, upheld the status quo even if the establishment didn't represent the social interests of the little guy. No, she guessed that her actions put her into closer association with Poison Ivy and Catwoman.

While she packed her panniers, she tried to come up with a moniker that fit her activism. Poison Ivy worked on behalf of plants while Catwoman stole to fund preserves that protect large predatory cats. Inez stopped packing and made a list of her hot button topics: Water, Monocultures, Pollinator Decline, Soil Erosion, Genetically Modified Food, Climate Change...The list was long. She wasn't as focused as either Catwoman or Poison Ivy.

She slumped in the standard issue dorm room desk chair. She felt overly complicated. She should simplify, pick a single cause to champion. The other students in the science department had all found their topic of interest, their discipline niche. She was sure that they also had roving diverse interests, but somehow they'd found peace in their academic foci.

Her advisor had told her that she'd feel better when she accepted that either she wasn't cut out for the rigidity and the depth of study needed to master a specific field or she'd switch into the Environmental Studies Department. In the Environmental Studies

Department, science was studied as if it were a branch of philosophy. Inez didn't want to study the action of others. She wanted action. Sitting around pondering the degradation of Earth's natural capital wouldn't solve anything. She wanted to be part of the solution, and she couldn't see Environmental Studies as part of that path.

Her bike was packed. She was ready to ride away from her campus life. However, she didn't know what to make of the lack of news about the water bottling plant. She was sure that someone would have picked up the story by now. The sun was up. Students were making their way across campus for classes. Checking the mirror, Inez felt she looked ready, despite her lack of sleep. However, she didn't know what she should be ready for.

The news was only covering the standard morning fare: politics, weather, local happenings, but not the water bottling plant. She started to wonder if she'd dreamed setting explosives in the pump room. Perhaps she'd forgotten a step and the charges hadn't detonated. Or, and now she was really worried, the explosion was being covered up, suppressed while Homeland Security collected evidence and tracked her down.

Inez really didn't believe that Homeland Security could cover up the deaths of the repair crew and the destruction of the pump room. The regular workers would have arrived hours ago and someone would have uploaded a picture or a video to the web or at least Tweeted about it or updated Facebook. The story should have gotten out by now, and at least one of the news organizations should be covering it.

By ten o'clock, Inez had had it. She had to know what had happened at the plant. She unplugged all of her electronics and left a note for her parents on the desk not to look for her. In the letter, she had explained that she'd taken a stance and had tried to change the world. She'd then pushed her bike down the stairs and out into the morning sun.

Her first stop would be the plant before riding northwest. Her plan was to ride North along Highway 75 and West along US 2 out of Michigan, through Wisconsin, and into Minnesota. In Minnesota, she'd look up the founder of the environmental club she fallen into at school. In the charter, Daniel Emmet Seward referred to an activist railroad that would keep people like her from going to jail. However, the charter was filled mostly with nonsense about taking responsibility, and actions unclaimed would be mistaken as wanton violence instead of as issue-based activism. Inez didn't care about the subtle nuances. She wanted the world to see the destruction of the plant, call attention to its existence. She'd hoped that journalists would pick up on older, forgotten stories about how the river had dried up downstream because of how much water the plant was using.

The lack of news coverage was simply unacceptable. She had to do something. Her first stop, she'd suddenly decided, wasn't going to be the plant, but to the student radio station.

Three

Inez walked into the student radio lab. She knew the morning DJ and reporters. A couple of them were involved in the environmental club. She had convinced herself that they'd allow her on for a few minutes before she disappeared forever. Seeing Andrew in the sound control booth, she waved.

Andrew, keeping one eye on the sound levels and signal strength, opened the booth door. "What's up?" He was wearing University of Michigan sweats. His hair was a web of thick dreadlocks. He motioned for her to take a seat and grab a cup of joe.

Inez wasn't one to banter or beat around the bush, so she said, "I need to make an announcement." She pointed into the studio where Heather and Phil were reading the news.

"Sure. What going on? The ECs having a fund raiser today?"

Inez cocked her head to one side and sipped the coffee. "Yeah, a bake sale." She lied.

"Cool." Andrew pulled out a pad of yellow legal-sized paper and pen. "Write it up and I'll feed it to Heather to include in our next round of campus updates." He went back to watching lights jump and dance across the monitors.

Inez took up the paper and the pen and wrote: *This just in: Inez Wick is wanted for questioning in conjunction with the late night bombing of the water bottling plant.* She took the pen and scratched what she'd written out. She tore the page off, balled the paper, and tossed into the recycling bin.

"Nice shot." Andrew said. "Don't worry about making your announcement sound good, just scribble down the facts. We'll do the rest."

"Sure." Inez tried again: *I set explosive charges in the pump room of the water-bottling factory out side of town. They were set to go off just after midnight last night.* She bit the pen before shredding the paper and tossing it into the bin with her first attempt.

"What?"

"I just can't find the right words."

"It's just a bake sale."

"Andy, when is a bake sale just a bake sale?"

"What's the issue this time?"

"Water."

"Water what? Clean water for developing countries? Water education for the locals? What?"

"Andy," Inez said, "I blew up the water-bottling factory outside town. I think that I might have killed some people."

Andrew's mouth opened as if he were going to say something. Instead, he rolled away in the wheeled office chair.

Using the moment, Inez stood up and took the microphone and switched it to ON. A moment of feedback made an appropriate prelude to her announcement. "Please excuse the interruption. I have taken over the radio station to bring you an important announcement. I, Inez Wick, set explosives at the water-bottling plant just outside town. They were set to detonate just after midnight. I don't know why there isn't anything on the news about the explosion and probable loss of life, but I do know that the factory steals precious clean water from flowing downstream. The factory must be stopped, and I took one step last night. I hope that you will pick up the cause and continue the fight using legal channels. That is all."

Inez switched off the microphone.

Andrew quickly reset the board. "Are you nuts?"

"No. I took a stand."

Andrew didn't say anything. He waved at Phil and Heather to pick where they'd stopped reading. "If what you said is true, you need to turn yourself into the police." He reached for the phone and dialed three numbers.

Inez backed out of the control room and left the radio station.

Four

Inez could hear the sirens and see the colored lights in the dark. She'd ridden all day and into the early night. She'd felt she'd gotten far enough away. For a moment, she'd considered going off road and into the woods on her bike. The cop car wouldn't be able to follow her into the trees. She'd then be able to double back along the river bank.

"Miss, please dismount your bike."

Inez laid her bike on the ground and slowly turned around. "Can I help you?"

"Do you have someplace you're going?"

"I was going to stop a few miles further north."

"It's getting dark. You're not supposed to ride along the highway."

"I have lights."

"Miss, it's the law."

"Oh." She tried batting her eyes and looking cute.

"Can I see some ID, preferably a driver's license?"

"It's in my bag."

The officer shined his light on her bag. He had his other hand on the handle of his holstered gun. "Please retrieve it."

She pulled out her wallet and handed over her license.

"While I look this up," he waved her license in the air, "you can sit in the back of the car."

"That's okay. Nice night."

He pointed the light in her eyes, blinding her momentarily. "I insist."

After he led her to the backseat, she asked, "Am I in trouble?"

"Please, this will only take a couple of minutes." He shut the door behind her before getting into the driver's seat. He scanned the barcode on the back of her license, and called in the stop.

Inez noticed that the doors were still unlocked. If she needed to, she'd be able to still make a run for it. She should have ridden off into the woods. The officer might not even have reported her. He might even have thought he'd seen a deer or something instead of biker.

Then she saw the officer look into the review mirror. She reached for the door. As she lifted up on the door's handle, the locks clicked into place.

Five

Inez sat in an interview room. She'd always imagined them having big one-way glass viewing windows like on TV, but this one was simply comprised of four concrete walls, a metal table, and three metal chairs. However, just like in the movies, two oddly paired men in dark suits sat across the table.

"My name's Agent Farth and this is Agent Ganies."

While Agent Farth was tall and lean, Agent Gaines was short and stocky. They were the proverbial odd couple. Agent Gaines had an athletic build, a full head of hair, and a pleasant smile. Meanwhile, Agent Farth was lean, malnourished, and bald.

Inez didn't say anything.

"We have you on tape at the water-bottling plant," said Agent Gaines. "And we have your radio confession."

A couple of minutes passed. Inez didn't speak, and the agents looked at her with hard, tired eyes. Before the silence got truly uncomfortable, Inez spoke up.

"What happens next?"

Agent Farth looked at Agent Gaines. "Well, that depends on you," said Agent Farth. "Do you know what happened at the plant?"

"No. Did anyone die?"

The agents looked at each other again.

"What?" Inez yelled. "Did I kill anyone? I didn't want anyone to die. I just…"

"No one's dead," said Agent Gaines, "Not even a scratch."

"Then they got out." Inez relaxed. She couldn't believe her luck.

Agent Farth stood and walked to the far corner of the room where he lit a cigarette. He took a couple of drags off it, which made him look even sicklier. "Your explosives failed to detonate, Miss Wick."

Her mouth hung open, and her shoulders slumped forward.

"Miss Wick, you looked relieved."

The room was quiet again. Agent Farth slowly filled the room with secondhand smoke. When he had finished his third cigarette in a row, Agent Gaines' coughing broke the silence.

"Give it a rest. Some of us still have our health, you know." Agent Gaines pulled a thick folder out of a black briefcase and set it on the table. He flipped it open. "Miss Wick, you're still in a lot of trouble. If you cooperate, we might see about a reduced sentence." He pointed at a photograph. "You know him?"

Curious, lifted her head. She knew man in the photograph. It was Daniel Emmet Seward. The man she had thought might be able to save her from prison. She nodded her head. "He founded the club."

Agent Gaines looked over his shoulder.

Agent Farth walked up to the table, put down a second folder, and opened it. "How about this guy?"

She looked, but she did know him. He had long black hair and hawkish features that hid tiny blue eyes. She shook her head. "No."

"You sure?" asked Agent Farth. "You've never seen him in the club's pictures, yearbooks, anything?"

"I don't know him." She leaned back. "Who is he?"

The agents looked at each other before opening even another file. This one was of a bike repairman in a shop somewhere. The guy looked old enough. The agents took a moment and arranged the photos in what looked like chronological order.

Agent Gaines pointed at the pictures. "What do you see?"

At first glance, the guy looked the same in every shot. After a few minutes of squinting, she saw it. In the tenth picture, not the ninth or the eleventh, the guy's eyes were blue instead of brownish-green in color. She then took a closer look at all the pictures, and she compared them to the photos in the other two files.

At last, she said, "It's Seward, only older." She shook her head. "Then," she picked up picture ten, "This isn't Seward." She looked at the other pictures, again. "This one's odd. The guy's not Seward. I think, but whoever he is, he looks like Seward."

The agents nodded.

Finding a bit of her confidence, knowing she hadn't killed anyone and the water-bottling plant was still intact, she asked, "What's this got to do with me?"

Agent Farth said, "You're going to help us catch him."

Beyond Peaking

One

Inez Wick sat down with a large bowl of popcorn. After a long day of work, she was ready to relax and think about something other than her boss's pending promotion, which would mean she'd likely have to do the work of two for several months. She poured a stiff rum and Coke and got ready to watch her favorite mysteries which were on tonight.

Inez didn't think it was odd that violent imagery, murder, and alcohol helped take the edge off an exhausting day. Instead of the gore, and if you asked her, the gore did bother her, she focused on the sexy, smart detectives and the workplace drama that emphasized right and wrong – catching the bad guys. Everyone, including the crime scene cleanup crews, were nothing but smiles. Inez's work place was full of ambiguity and sullen expressions.

About halfway into her first mystery, a reporter interrupted. "Sorry for the interruption. We go live, now, to the White House for coverage of what we have been told will be a turning point in American history. No wait, world history." The reporter looked pale and unprepared. "We've been told that in just a few seconds we will be addressed by the president." There was a strange pause as the reporter listened, putting his hand over his left ear. He looked into the camera and sternly said, "We go live to the White House."

Inez didn't believe that anything this president had to say was important enough to interrupt her mysteries. As she waited on the couch, too tired to get up, too depressed to even try and change the channel, she started thinking about work. What was going to happen? Should she apply for her boss's job when her boss got the promotion? She didn't want to have to work under anyone else. Her current boss was a good boss. She listened to Inez's input and took it seriously. Inez thought they worked well together, and she didn't want the team to separate. Besides, it had been a long time since Inez had had a good boss, and she felt she'd already had her fair share of terrible ones.

The president sat in the Oval Office, but Inez had tuned him out. He wasn't her president. Her president would have respected the sanctity of evening mysteries. However, she sat up and paid attention when she heard the words, "gas prices," because she commuted an hour each direction, to and from work, and the trip was too expensive at $2.75 a gallon.

The president continued: "OPEC and the oil industry, either in an attempt to keep the price artificially low or in ignorance so complete, have lied to the American people. They have lied to the world. I deeply wish that I had better news, but we – the human race – have..."

In her pajamas, Inez pushed aside her popcorn and grabbed the keys to her car. She was seeing an environmental economist a couple times a week. He was a cutie, but he was depressing and overly serious about the state of the world's natural capital, whatever the fuck that was. What he did have going for him, besides his looks, was a deep voice that caused Inez to dream of better tomorrows on sandy beaches. She hung on every word he spoke. One night, he had told her over dinner that if the president ever said "OPEC" and "lied" in a national address, she'd only have a few minutes to act.

Inez couldn't believe that her boyfriend was right about all this fossil fuel mumbo-jumbo. She had wanted to stick around and listen to the end of the presidential address, but she had taken her boyfriend's advice and driven to the nearest store. She felt lucky as she stood in line at Wal-Mart that Wal-Mart was only just down the street. She was drawing attention from other shoppers, but she knew what she was doing was right.

The cashier asked, "How many? I can just scan one, if that's all you got in your cart."

"Twenty. I could only fit twenty in the cart." Inez put hand over her mouth. "What if twenty isn't enough?"

"Ma'am, I've never seen anyone buy more than one at a time."

Inez nodded and paid with her credit card. She hated credit cards and used it only for absolute emergencies. She couldn't think of a bigger emergency than this one, but she still hated the feeling of the potential interest accruing if she didn't pay it all off at once.

After loading her car, Inez noticed that the streets were still quiet. She was having a hard time understanding why no one was on the move. Was she just that far ahead of everyone else? When she saw her boyfriend again, she would have to thank him. She was sure that he was out doing the same thing right now. She thought of calling him until she realized that as she hurried out of the house she'd left her cell phone on the coffee table in front of the TV. Inez pulled into the first gas station she came across.

The Shell station was empty. Inez didn't understand what was taking everyone so long, but their hesitation was in her favor. First, she filled up her car. Then, she slowly, carefully filled up each of the twenty, four-gallon tanks she'd just bought from Wal-Mart. Filling all twenty went faster than Inez had expected. After replacing the pump, she watched the small, gray and black screen. When the screen was finished asking her if she'd like a carwash, coffee, or cheap cigarettes, she selected "Yes" for a receipt. Her receipt read as she expected it would read: $2.75 per gallon.

After loading her car and pulling out into the street, she stopped at the light. Inez could see, down the hill into the valley, headlights pulling out from driveways. She thought she could hear angry car horns in the distance. Still waiting for the light to turn, she happened to looked in her review mirror. The Shell sign that had just read $2.75 per gallon, now read: "Closed. Gas Reserved. Homeland Security."

Two

Inez pulled into her driveway. She waited for the garage door to open fully before parking. She looked around her small, one car garage. The garage was clean. Except for her bike, a Big Dummy touring cycle built by *Surly*, stored in the corner near the door, the garage was empty.

Whenever Inez looked around her garage, a choking sadness would paralyze her. A garage needed a man, or so she often thought. A man would line the walls of a garage with tools for fixing, cutting, painting, and trouble making. When she'd first bought the house, she had sat in the garage. On the floor, she had imagined greasy, woody, manly smells. At that moment, she'd promised herself to reserve this sacred space for a man as if she could pick one up at Home Depot as easily as a screwdriver or monkey wrench. Years passed, and Inez had been unsuccessful at furnishing her garage with a man. A niche she hoped to fill soon. Perhaps her environmental economist, she'd thought as of late, but as many times as she had thought about asking him to move in with her, she'd also dismissed him as a kook.

Now, standing in her garage, next to her car overloaded with twenty, four-gallon canisters of 87 grade gasoline, Inez could barely bring herself to pick a corner to stack them. Every inch of space she claimed in the garage seemed to eat away at the reserved space, dwindled her hope of ever fully, correctly furnishing it with a man.

Inez picked the back wall of the garage. Once she'd chosen the location, unloading the red canisters went quickly and easily. She stacked them five long and four high. When finished unloading, she stood back and marveled at probably the last eighty gallons of gas she'd likely be able to afford. While she marveled, another more sinister thought crawled over her skin in the form of goose bumps.

Inez put her hands over her mouth, "I have to hide them." She spun around. "How long has the garage door been open?" She walked outside and half way down her driveway. She looked both right and left. Seeing no one, she returned inside and closed the garage door.

Still, something was quivering around in the pit of her stomach. An audible gurgling noise caused Inez to put a hand over stomach. "Not now. Pull it together." She grabbed one of the canisters of gas and went inside the house.

Inside, she walked in through the kitchen immediately dismissing her cupboards and under the sink as too small. Only one or two at the most would have fit. Next, she paused in the living room. The TV was still on, and of course, she was missing her favorite show. "Focus."

She opened and shut the closets in the hall, the bathroom, and her bedroom. Her closets were full. She wondered, just for a second, if there was room in her life for a man. Her closets were ordered and neat. She knew just where to find any item she needed. Unless what she was looking for had been misplaced or lost, which always seemed to be the case. If she had to look, that needed item was lost.

She stopped in the hall. She looked up and pulled down the stepladder that led up into the attic. She poked her head though the trapdoor. It was hot in the attic, hotter than it was outside and on the first floor. The attic didn't have lights. The only light came from a small, round, south facing window.

Ever since moving in, Inez had wanted to do something with the attic. She knew that a few of the other houses on her street had basements. Some of which were finished and fully furnished. However, it rained so often that her neighbors were always complaining about water damage and pumping, always pumping. Inez was glad her house didn't have a basement to flood, but it meant that her house was smaller than most of the others on the block. There were rumors that the woman who'd owned it before her had been alone all her life and blamed it on the size of her home.

Inez's home was small for Cherrywood Lane: three bedrooms, a living room, a kitchen/dining room, and only one bathroom. The number of bathrooms in each house on Cherrywood Lane determined status. Not the number rooms or the size of the kitchen or how ornamental the den was, but number of bathrooms. However, it wasn't only the quantity of bathrooms, because the Morgan's and the Driver's both had five, but the size and function that set the Driver's a part.

Mr. Driver had designed the master bath with his third wife in mind. He had joined it to the master bedroom in two ways, or so the rumor went. The first was typical, a door. There was nothing special about the door. However, the walk-in rain-room shower shared a see-through Plexiglas wall. On the bedroom side of the wall, the shower was obscured by a thick black curtain that could be, and often was, parted, so Mr. Driver could view Mrs. Driver lather up.

The thought of such an arrangement did more for Inez than the steamy vampire romances she devoured. Mr. Driver was handsome, and on more than one occasion, she'd fantasized about putting on a personal performance for him. Inez could see Mr. Driver's home, down the street from hers, through the small round window in her attic. Every time she saw the house, thoughts of his master bath filled her consciousness. Soon, however, the weight of the canister brought her back to the task at hand.

She found a corner in the back of the attic. It was cooler than it was near the window, but it was still much warmer than it was in the garage or in the house. Inez felt she needed to hide the gas somewhere. She couldn't make it easy for looters to steal it, and she felt it wouldn't take long for looters to check her garage, perhaps even siphon the gas out of her car.

"No one will look in the attic." Inez smiled. She'd worry about better ventilation later. For now, she just needed somewhere to keep her supply safe. It took another nineteen trips, but Inez managed to move all twenty canisters into the attic. She hadn't been able to keep to just one corner. The slope of her roof would only allow the canisters to be stacked two high in the corner, so they spilled out along one wall. At the apex of the roof, she'd been able to stack them four high.

Looking at her watch, she shrieked, "Five minutes." If nothing else went wrong tonight, she'd still be able to catch *Law and Order*.

Settling on the couch, her drink and popcorn were where she'd left them. She picked up her remote and flipped channels. Setting her remote down next to her cell phone, she noticed that she had a missed call.

Three

Checking her missed call log, Inez saw she'd missed three calls from her mother, one from her father, one from the environmental economist she was seeing, and one from Joan, her best girlfriend. Not one of them had left her a message, so she put her phone down believing that if they really wanted to talk they'd have left her a message, texted her, or would call back soon enough that she didn't have to worry. Besides, she still needed to relax. Tomorrow was another day after all, and she knew it was only going to be longer because she was going to have to ride her bike.

Riding her bike meant going to bed soon and missing her late night mystery reruns. Some of her friends had asked her how she could watch and re-watch whodunits repeatedly. Didn't she remember the plot? While Inez couldn't understand how they could remember such things or why they'd want to remember them. If she'd remembered the solutions to the mysteries, she'd wouldn't enjoy watching them a second or third time, so Inez made an effort to forget.

As her mystery transitioned from the detectives to the prosecutors, her phone rang: a peaceful wind over water sound accented with the chirping of insects, frogs, and the occasional bird. Inez looked at the face she'd assigned to the number flash on the phone's screen: her mother wagging her finger. Inez pushed the popcorn bowl away, muted the TV, and answered the phone.

"Yeah, Ma."

"Is that anyway to answer the phone: 'Yeah, Ma'?"

"Yeah. Mother."

"Are you still single? Perhaps, it's how you answer the phone."

"You know where I work. Would you prefer I answer, 'Thank you for calling Inez Wick's house. How can I direct your call?"

"You know what I mean. Maybe if you'd try a…"

"Mom, why'd you call?"

"Okay, I just think that…"

"I'll hang up."

"Inez, honey, I have to get to the store in the morning to refill a couple of my medications. Can you take me?"

Inez stood up. She paced as she talked. "Why can't you take the bus? You always take the bus." Inez paused, waiting for a response. Nothing. "Or you could have your meds delivered. You never wanted my help. What's up? What's really going on?" She sat on the floor her back to the couch. "Oh God. You're dying. You're dying aren't you?"

"Heavens no. What's going on over there? You okay, dear?"

"Well, what then?" Inez was back on her feet and walking laps around the couch and the coffee table.

"Didn't you hear? It was all over the news."

"What?"

"You were watching one of your murder shows and missed it."

Through the phone, Inez could hear her mother take in a deep breath, which meant that her mother was about to nag.

"Those shows you watch. They're filth. Someone always gets killed, and someone's always lying about doing it. I just can't see why you…"

"Mother! Why'd you call?"

"I said that already. I need my meds. I need you. I need my daughter to get me my meds. Stop yelling at me."

"But I don't understand. Why now?"

"Because I'm running out."

"No." Inez laid down on the couch. Her mother had never asked for help before tonight, and when Inez had offered to come around and help out, her mother had pushed her away. Her mother had claimed that if Inez started hanging around old people, Inez would forget what young people should be doing: getting married and having babies. "Why do you want my help now? Why do you want me around, now?" Inez was starting to tear up.

"You really don't know what's going on outside. Okay, honey, brace yourself. You sitting down?"

"Yes."

"The president, you know, our president, of the United States, he was just on the TV talking about Saudi Arabia and the Middle East being out of oil. They pumped their last barrel yesterday, and they didn't tell anyone until this afternoon." She continued without taking a breath. "Then he went on to say that all non-military reserves had been depleted under the previous administration, so he's put all gas stations under federal lockdown, claiming national security. He's also putting a stop on all non-essential personal automobile use. However, he said he couldn't and wouldn't stop anyone from driving, but he suggested restraint – 'to drive only in the case of an emergency.' Then he went on to say, he had a plan for the future, but it would take everyone working together. "

It seemed like her mother had finished recounting the broadcast, so Inez asked, "So you need a ride to get your meds?"

"That's what I've been trying to say."

"Well, if the president said…"

"Fuck him. I need my meds. You need to pick me up, so I can get more. I can't run out."

Inez hadn't ever, not once, in her life heard her mother curse. "I'll be there at seven, okay. Will seven work? I mean, we could go yet tonight. Walgreens…"

"Seven will be fine. I'll be ready."

The phone went silent. Her mother had hung up. Inez watched her mother's face and the number of minutes she was on the phone blink then fade as the phone went back to standby.

She got up off the couch and made her way to bed. Exhausted, she immediately fell into a restless sleep, plagued with dreams of tomorrow.

Four

Inez didn't really want to waste the gas on her mother, which if she thought about it for more than a couple of seconds, made her sound selfish. However, as she turned the key in the car's ignition, she felt her selfishness turn into righteousness. She was going to have to tell her mother that this was going to be the last trip to the store. Gas was too precious now.

Driving through the ill-designed roads of her suburb, Inez found the highway deserted of traffic. She checked the clock on the dash: It read just before six. The highway should have been filled with commuters trying to get to work by seven, eight, or nine depending how far they had to travel. The road was too quiet, as if the entire world had agreed to say home and play hooky.

The streets and avenues leading up to her mother's retirement center were as equally quiet. Cars and trucks were parked curbside, like fossils waiting for the soil to churn them under for eternity. Still, Inez thought there would be people out walking or riding bicycles. She couldn't figure why the world should have ground to a halt.

Inez parked her car in the cul-de-sac in front of the center. The flower garden was beautiful. The yellow rose bushes that Inez had donated to center were in full bloom. Her bushes looked wonderful, so Inez didn't care that her mother had said they were a waste of money because her mother didn't plan on staying long. Inez could never bring herself to talk about her mother's eventual death as her mother wanted. Her mother would poke her bony finger into Inez's side and say, "I'm going soon. Be ready." How was Inez supposed to 'be ready' for her mother's death? Was Inez supposed to practice in front of the mirror: "Goodbye, Mom. I love you."

Inez turned the car's engine off and texted her mother, "I'm here. You ready?"

Her mother texted back, "Down in a second."

It amazed Inez how quickly her mother had learned to use a cell phone. Inez bought her mother the latest and greatest do-everything phone on the market. At first, her mother had been upset about the cost and claimed no use for such a device. Now, the phone never left her side.

Inez's mother had discovered a vibrant community through her phone's "Seniors Do" app. While, Inez's father watched sports all day every day, Inez's mother was usually out meeting up with the "sDos." Just last week, Inez's mother had claimed to have gone skydiving. There were pictures as proof. Skydiving! However, the new phone had caused a few problems too.

Inez watched as her mother waved. One of the "keepers," as her mother referred to the on location nurses, stood in the doorway. In all white, he waved back as Inez's mother climbed into the car.

"Go!" Her mother yelled.

Inez started the car and pulled out into the street. After turning the corner, she asked, "What was that all about?"

"Don't you know?"

"I must not." Inez turned again. A Wal-Mart wasn't too far, but far away enough that she could understand her mother's hesitation to walk. They'd pull in soon enough.

"It's not safe." Her mother paused. She pulled out her phone and pushed something on the screen. Then she scrolled down a ways. "According to today's paper, people have been killed...Wait. I mean, people are being killed for what's in their gas tank." She put her phone down and looked out her window. She moved her head slowly, watching for would be attackers.

"Relax. I haven't seen anyone on the street this morning. Where are those headlines from?"

"Today's paper, I told you."

"*The Local?*"

"Yes, *The Local.*"

"That rag. I've asked you to stop reading it. It's not a newspaper. Did you believe it when they *reported* aliens had landed, and they were demanding humanity turn over its supply of Twinkies?"

"No. That story was in the funny section. The one today is in the News-as-it-happens section. I trust it."

Inez turned into the Wal-Mart parking lot. Inez's mother pulled out her handicapped review hanger, and she hung it.

Inez snickered, "I don't think that we're going to need that today."

"Park next to the door then, I don't want to walk much this morning. My knees are killing me."

Inez pulled into the space next to the door and turned off the car. As she was about to open her door, her mother stopped her.

"Don't."

"We need to go inside."

"No." Her mother pointed with her age-warped index finger. "You stay with the car."

"Why?"

"In case. Just in case." Her mother opened the door, "Stay," and she quickly went into the store.

Inez wanted to stand and stretch her legs. She got out of the car and walked around back where she leaned against the trunk. She hadn't slept well. She had too real dreams about the gas canisters she'd hidden away in the attic. One had ended with her home exploding in flames. One had started out with looters searching her house while one of them raped her. One had been a tryst with Mr. Driver in exchange for a canister. Regardless of the content, each of her dreams had ended with her waking up and looking at the red glowing numbers of her alarm clock. Only one of those dreams seemed remotely possible, and Inez hoped that Mr. Driver was game for it. Still, Inez promised herself that she'd move the canisters again today.

She retrieved her phone and took a picture of the parking lot. Wal-Mart was open twenty-four/seven, and the parking lot was never empty. Today, however, it was completely desolate. Looking at the picture she'd just taken, Inez realized it was of just an empty parking lot. If anyone was going to believe the lot belonged to Wal-Mart, she was going to have to take another one from an alternative vantage point.

Inez abandoned the car and walked out into Wal-Mart's parking lot.

Five

She stopped walking and turned around to take a picture from the other end of the parking lot. Again, Inez was struck with how quiet and peaceful the world was without cars. She held up her phone and took a couple of quick shots. Then, in a fit of inspiration, she narrated a short video: "This is Inez Wick, reporting from Wal-Mart's parking lot the day after the end of oil. As you can see by the superstore's vacant lot, people are choosing to not to drive today. What will this mean for the US Economy? If people can't get to work, can't get to the store, and can't get…"

As Inez panned her phone over the parking lot, she saw someone trying to break into her car. Through her phone, Inez couldn't make out the figure. She could tell, however, that who ever it was he or she was trying to rip open the flap that covered her gas tank.

Inez didn't immediately know how to react. She started by putting her phone back into her purse. She didn't run towards her car. Instead, she walked. She was going to keep her cool. Perhaps, if she didn't provoke the thief, everything would turn out for the best. Besides, whoever was trying to break in to her gas tank was doing a piss poor job of it.

Before Inez could confront the thief, Inez's mother came out of Wal-Mart holding large white prescription bags in each hand. Her mother started running towards the car arms outstretched like a bomber about to obliterate an enemy camp.

"Get! Get!" Her mother yelled as if trying to shoo a dog before it was able to complete its business. "Get away from there, you! That's my daughter's car."

The hooded figure was tall and heavyset. Inez was close enough to see that she didn't want to approach the situation in the same way as her mother. However, Inez had to act quickly before her mother got hurt.

Taking her keys out of her purse, she tried the keyless ignition. Before today, Inez had never tried it. She just didn't see the point of starting the car without her inside at the wheel. The salesman had convinced her to upgrade by telling her that she'd never have to endure a freezing cold or burning hot car again. All she'd have to do was start her car remotely with her key fob a minute or two before she wanted to depart. Inez could only have wished to have been that organized and on the ball.

As the car started, both her mother and the hooded thief jumped and looked around as if they'd been caught with a hand in a cookie jar. Seeing Inez calmly walking toward the car, the hooded individual took off around the corner.

Inez ran to the car.

Six

"What were you doing out of the car?" Inez's mother asked, hands still in the air holing her prescription bags. "I told you to stay."

Inez ignored her mother. She opened the door and slid behind the wheel. Next, she reached over and unlocked her mom's door. "Come on. We've got to go." Inez couldn't sit still. She kept bouncing in her seat. How long did it take to get in the car? "Come on."

As soon as her mother had shut the door, Inez backed out of the parking space and took off through the lot.

"Slow down. You're going to get a ticket, us killed, or both." A line her mother used often while in the passenger's seat over the years. "He's gone. I think that you can slow down."

Inez checked her review mirror. She didn't see anyone coming after her. The streets were as quiet and as abandoned as they were on their way to the store. Inez relaxed a little. She let her shoulders sag in relief. "Sorry. I just didn't think. I mean, there was no one around. The parking lot was completely empty." Keeping her eyes on the road and nervously checking and rechecking the review, she continued. "I'm surprised you were even able to get service. I mean, who was there to help you? No one was in the lot. I wanted a picture. I..."

"Honey, the Mexicans don't drive cars. They can't afford them."

Inez's mouth hung open. She'd never heard a hateful or racist word come from her mother. "Mom."

"What? It's true." Her mother resumed watching the road. "The young man who helped me said as much."

"Still," Inez pushed, "Mexicans drive cars too. What's with the sweeping generalization?" Besides her mother's lack of tact, Inez was starting to calm down after the assault on her car. She started to wonder, why her car when there were hundreds of thousands of cars, if not millions in the city parked curbside down any side street. It wasn't like all the cars hand suddenly vanished after the president's speech last night. To prove to herself that cars hadn't vanished, she turned a block early and went down a side street. "Who helped you in the store, again? I'm sorry, I missed what you just said."

Inez's mother had been speaking. She started her story over. "The nicest Mexican boy greeted me at the door. You know, I hated it when old people greeted. They're depressing. If I wanted to see old people, I wouldn't leave the home. Damn old people, and their wrinkled skin and bad knees." Her mother shook her head before continuing. "He, the Mexican boy, took me back to the pharmacy where he explained that the pharmacist wasn't going to make it in today, but he had keys and was going to school for pharmacology. He said he could help me if I'd trust him."

Inez was horrified. Did her mother get the correct medications? She couldn't believe what she was hearing.

"I didn't have much choice. Things are only going to get worse you know. We're lucky we went today."

Inez, as if for the first time, noticed the size of the bags her mother had at her feet. "What did you get?"

"Everything, Honey. I cleaned them out."

Inez couldn't think of a time she'd seen her mother look so happy. No, happy wasn't right. No, she looked devilishly sadistic. "You mean it?"

"Yeah, I have enough to last months, perhaps the year. I got all my meds."

"How'd you pay?" Inez knew, because she often helped with her medical expenses, that the drugs were the bulk of her mother's expenditures. Just one of her mother's painkillers ran several hundred a month after insurance, and her mother was on at least three types of medications to keep her heart healthy, her blood flowing and clean, and her liver from swelling.

"I didn't."

Inez put her foot down, reactively, and turned to look her mother in the eyes. Inez was going to get the truth. "Was there a Mexican boy or did you just help yourself behind the drug counter?"

"You're in the middle of an intersection."

She didn't care. There were no cars on the road anyway. "I'm not budging until you tell me the truth." Inez couldn't believe that she was having a conversation about shoplifting with her mother as if her mother were an unknowing three year old.

Before her mother could answer, a large truck plowed into the rear passenger's side of the Inez's car, sending it into a spin.

Seven

Inez's hands were tied together behind her back. She lay on her side in the grass. Dew soaked her left side. She watched the hooded figure from Wal-Mart's parking lot through squinted eyes. The hooded figure was male, which was what she had figured. However, he couldn't have been older than thirteen or fourteen. He was linebacker big, but he didn't look like he shaved and his skin shimmered with pubescent silk.

Inez tried to spot her mother, but she could only see her car, the kid and his truck, and the empty streets. How long had she been unconscious? Would emergency responders be right around the corner or was she on her own? Regardless, she had do something.

"Hey!" she yelled, rolling to a sitting positing. "Oooo." Her head throbbed, and her neck wouldn't straighten. Instead, her left ear seemed pined to her shoulder.

The kid turned around. He threw his chin out in a "what's up" acknowledgement before returning to Inez's car.

"Is my mom…"

"She's over there." He turned around again and pointed to the curb. "She didn't make it." He shrugged his shoulders, and he returned to her car.

Inez turned her body so that she could look where the kid had pointed. Her mother lay face down in the grass. Her limbs were limply askew and lifeless. Her hair was matted with a red-brown stain that ran into the grass, down the curb, and into the gutter. Inez choked down bile as it tried to escape her mouth.

She tried to stand, but she was too dizzy and fell to her knees. Suddenly, a hand gripped her shoulder.

"You have to think about you now." He pushed her back onto the wet grass. "No one's coming."

"Why?" Was all Inez could whimper.

He looked confused as if she had asked him a riddle with a difficult answer. His blue eyes were distant and a few wrinkles crossed his forehead and around the sides of his nose. "Yeah, bitch.

Because I can." He slapped her hard across the face. "Look around you." He stood. Hands raised, he spun around. "No gas. No police. No people." He made a gun with his pointer finger and his thumb. He pointed it at Inez's head. "Bang, bitch. No one cares. They're all glued to the tube." He started to leave.

"Wait. What about me?"

He turned around, play gun made out of his hand, again pointed at her head. He looked her up and down slowly. Instead of play shooting her again, he made a V with both hands, thrust out his crotch. He slapped his upper thighs in a grotesquely obvious gesture, telegraphing his intentions.

"Is it gas you want?" Inez struggled up onto her knees. "You want gas, right? Gas?" Her cheek was starting to swell from where he had hit her. However, her head was free from her shoulder. Tears welling up, she said, "I can get you gas."

The kid ignored her.

Slowly this time, she got to her feet. She leaned into a tree for support. She looked down the sidewalk. She could see her mother's retirement home. She was half a block away. Wobbling a little, she looked down the street in the other direction, nothing but houses. The curtains were drawn and doors were shut, but Inez knew that someone was home in each one. The houses were closer. She turned and bolted.

Her run toward the small red and yellow house was a labored stagger and limp. The house's sidewalk was lined with a knee-high white picket fence and rose bushes. Roses peeked over the top and though railings. Inez stumbled, brushing her leg against a flower with quarter inch long thorns that tore into her flesh. She screamed.

A tall man, who looked to be in his mid thirties, opened the white door. Other than being tall, he wasn't muscular. He wore thick glasses that were semi-hidden under long greasy bangs. The t-shirt he wore read: BITE ME and pictured a dog chewing on a pixilated 3.14... in the shape of pie dish.

Inez continued to limp down his path to the door. "Help me," she screamed. "Help me."

The tall man stood behind the screen door, unmoving. His facial expression was unreadable and distorted by the mesh in the storm door. He didn't call back to her.

The kid caught up with Inez. He put his hand in her hair and pushed her to the ground. He kicked her in the side. Next, he turned to he tall man behind the screen door. "Fuck off."

The tall man slowly shut his door.

"See bitch." The kid pointed at the closed door. "No gas. No police. No help for you." He grabbed hold of her hair again. This time he pulled her toward the street. "You say you've got gas." He pushed her ahead of him. "I took your gas."

"I have more."

"I checked the trunk." He kicked her again. "Where?"

"Home. At home."

He opened the passenger's door to his truck and pushed Inez inside. His truck was old enough to have a bench seat. The vinyl was hot from the summer sun and burned against Inez's legs. She squirmed until the kid hit her again. This time he hit her with his fist square on the side of her head. Her head bounced off the back of the seat before she crumpled into a ball under the dash.

"Calm the fuck down." He shut the door and walked around the other side. After getting in and starting up the truck, he said, "Address."

At first, Inez didn't answer. Her head was ringing so badly that the rest of the world was muffled. She could see that the kid wanted something. She guessed. "Home."

"Address." He raised his arm as if to backhand her.

She tried to become smaller. The distance between his looming fist and where she sat on the floor seemed to enlarge, but as the distance increased, the kid's arm also seemed to lengthen. She mumbled.

"Yeah," he smiled and pulled away from the curb, "I know that neighborhood."

Eight

Finding her nerve, Inez climbed on to the bench seat. Hands still tired, she sat with her back to the passenger's side door. Sniffling, she said, "I'm Inez."

The kid looked at her as he took the exit to her neighborhood. He smiled, and his teeth showed bits of glossy metal spelling: NEIL. He winked before focusing on the on the roads. He wasn't stopping at lights and completely ignored signs.

The streets were still empty. Doors were closed. The over athletic were not out walking their dogs. Children were not on their way to school. It was as if the entire world had collectively decided to take the day off in mourning, eerily celebrating the end of an era.

However, in the absence of people and cars, suddenly, other forms of life attempted to take center stage.

As Neil and Inez turned the corner, Neil slammed on the brakes. The truck skidded to a halt. Neil had his seatbelt fastened. Inez flew off the seat. Her head cracked the windshield but didn't shatter it.

After watching a gaggle of Canadian Geese and their newborn goslings finish crossing the road, he reached across Inez's body and unlatched the passenger's side door. He opened it and then pushed Inez out with his foot. "Bitch, good riddance."

The impact with the pavement woke Inez. She instinctively rolled but in the wrong direction. Instead of rolling away from Neil's truck, she rolled under the back tire. As the truck pulled away, Inez didn't even have enough left in her to scream as Neil drove over her leg. Unconsciousness took her again.

Nine

Inez woke. She sat up straight in bed then immediately reaching for her calf muscles, screamed. Her face was flush, puffy, and wet with tears. The knot in her calf balled, painfully contorting her muscle. Sniffling and trying to take her mind of her knotted calf muscle, she thought about her prickly legs and needing to shave them in the morning. Breathing deeply, she looked at the green numbers on the alarm clock.

"Shit," she said.

The pain subsided, but Inez still felt as if she'd truly been run over by a truck. Gingerly, she put pressure on her legs as she slid out of bed. Turning off her alarm clock, which was about to sound, she remembered that she'd promised to take her mother to Wal-Mart to fulfill her prescriptions last night. If she didn't hurry, she'd be late. Her mother hated waiting.

The shower felt good, but she wasn't going to get to wear a skirt to work today. She felt her legs again while drying them. Nope. She was doomed to don slacks, one more fault for her mother to criticize. Inez could hear it now: *To get a man, you need to show your legs. Men like legs, Inez.* Her mother would then reach for her knee and pinch her harder than her mother's bony dry hands should be able to muster. Just thinking about it caused her calf muscle to twitch.

"Fuck." She quickly sat on the toilet. Putting her face in her hands, she took long slow breaths as her leg continued to twitch.

After a couple of minutes, she made her way back to her bedroom. There, she pulled out a simple black pair of slacks, flats, and a white blouse. Distracted, she put her blouse on with out first donning a bra. Inez shook her head. She could see her nipples through the faux-silk. Just for a second, she thought about what her mother would think. Her mother would probably call her a slut or worse. Inez just couldn't win with her mother.

Her mother wouldn't let up until Inez was married and had put her "baby-machine" to work producing grandchildren. Her mother never failed to express a desire to see grandchildren before she passed.

Inez wanted kids. She wanted three or four of them, but she wasn't going to settle for some pretty-boy who made her laugh. No,

Inez wanted a real man: a man that would provide for this family while she raised their children at home. Inez felt sheepish when she thought about how traditionally sexist her domestic views were. Her environmental economist was fun to be around as long as he didn't fall prey to apocalyptic visions of ecological doom. However, he taught at a local technical college where he barely made thirty thousand a year. He'd never be able to support her household fantasies alone, which would mean she'd either have to work or pass on him all together. As she dug for a clean white bra, her thoughts were leaning towards *pass*.

She was going to have to skip breakfast. She longingly looked at the coffee pot and the spoiling fruit for smoothies on the counter. Pausing, she called her mother.

"Yeah."

"Mom, is that anyway to answer the phone?"

"You should talk. Are you here? I'll be right down."

"Mom!" Inez looked at her phone. The time she'd talked flashed then disappeared. "Shit. Shit, shit, shit." Well, at least what to do about breakfast had been decided. On the way out the door, she grabbed her purse and couple of folders of work she'd not gotten to because she'd been out stocking up on gas.

For a short second, Inez thought about all those canisters in the attic.

Ten

For a morning after a major presidential announcement about the state of gas imports, the roads sure were crowded. Inez had dreamed something completely different. She had imagined complete desolation, but rush hour was rush hour. People had to get to work, and the only way out of the suburbs into the city was a car on the highway.

As she changed lanes, she dialed her mother again.

Her mother picked up, "Where are you?"

"Stuck in traffic."

"I thought you were in the loop waiting for me. How far away are you?"

"Ten minutes. There are flashing lights up ahead, so maybe longer. If you want I'll text you when I get there." Inez bought her car to a full stop. She tried to see around the SUV in font of her, but she couldn't get a good angle to view what was going on up ahead. "Yeah. Mom, I'm stuck."

"You should have left earlier. What if you're late for work? You can't lose your job, not right now."

"I know, mom. I'll call them next."

"Okay."

"I'll see you soon." Her words were interrupted with static. She looked at her phone and saw that her mother had hung up on her, again. "Always on your terms," Inez thought.

Instead of calling work, she dialed her environmental economist. She waited through a couple of rings before considering disconnecting. "Pony up, Inez," she said aloud.

His answering service picked up, "You've reached Anthony Heartwood, instructor, author, and freelance journalist, please leave a message including a call back number." The service beeped.

Traffic still at a dead stop, Inez left a short, practiced message, "Tony, it's over. You're a nice guy, but I need something more. Please don't call. Oh, and thanks for the advice: I bought twenty four-gallon canisters of gas last night before the feds closed the station. Bye." She hung up and looked at her phone. She'd done it. She'd broken up with Tony.

A smile crossed her face, and traffic started moving again. Her day was looking up. Now all she had to do was endure her mother for a few minutes this morning before work. Yeah, she could endure.

Now that she'd broken it off with Tony, Mr. I'm-so-depressed-about-everything, she felt free to pursue Mr. Downs at work. The irony of his last name didn't escape her; however, he was a VP, and he'd been eyeing her lately. She didn't know if he was married, but she'd get to bottom of that question as soon as she got to work.

Pulling into the loop in front of her mother's retirement center, Inez experienced a sensation not unlike déjà vu. As she slowed, she saw a shadowy version of her car pulling away. Inside, Inez could have sworn that she could see her and her mother arguing, but the image dissipated as it exited the loop.

Inez parked. She picked up her phone and texted her mother, "I'm here."

Her mother texted back, "About time. I'll be right down."

Eleven

On their way back from Wal-Mart, Inez's mother said, "How's Tony? Any progress?"

Inez, focusing on the road, ignored her mother.

"He called this morning."

"What?" Inez looked at her mother, eyes wide. She was now completely alert, and she wished that traffic would come to a stop, but morning traffic southbound was always light.

"He couldn't get a hold of your father." She let slide a few choice words about his manhood, ending with, "…may he die soon."

Inez knew better than to interrupt her mother when she got in one of her moods over Inez's father, so she suppressed a snicker. Inez thought her mother was cute when she got all riled up and swore at someone other than her, even if was her father. After fifty-years of marriage and a painful separation, Inez thought her mother was allowed a few raw nerves. However, she wanted to know why Tony had called.

"Tony called?"

"He did."

"Are you going to tell me?"

Her mother laid her hands in her lap, settling in as if to tell an epic tale of love and war circa the fall of Troy. "Well, at first we chatted. He is such a nice man. He cares about things that no one else would stop to consider. He's handsome, too. I hope you haven't gone and done something stupid. It'd be so like you to fuck this up. So like you."

"Fuck what up? Mom, what did he want?"

"After we talked; Oh, by the way, he called as soon as I got off the phone with you his morning." Her mother, in a bizarrely caring gesture, put her hand on Inez's leg. "He asked me if he could ask you to marry him." Then she pinched Inez's leg, "Don't you fuck this up for me. I want grandbabies. You hear me? Grandbabies before I die."

Twelve

Inez watched her mother as she walked into the retirement center. What was she going to do about Tony? She knew deep down that she'd done the right thing by calling it off with Tony. Still, she'd broken with up his voicemail. If he had planned on popping the question, he'd want to see her. He'd want to talk. He always wanted to talk. He was a modern man, liked to discuss his feelings and listen to her. At first, she'd like that quality and encouraged it in him. However, she soon realized that what she needed was a stoic man who got up and went to work, came home for dinner, had a beer or two before bed, and above all else, kept his feelings about unimportant shit to himself. If she'd wanted to listen to someone go on about this-that-and-whatever-else, she'd have continued to date women.

However, she was already late for work. On the highway, she turned on the radio. She needed something to take her mind off Tony, her mother's baby imperative, and work. National Public Radio usually did the trick, and perhaps they'd discuss the president's address. By the number of cars and trucks on the road, she felt like she'd dreamed it all, but while at Wal-Mart with her mother, she re-discovered receipts from her jaunt to the Shell station.

The morning news cycle was beginning to re-start. "Good," thought Inez. Traffic was still slow into the city. She'd likely get to hear the entire segment. Secretly, she hoped that she'd still be in car for the *Morning Market Report*. She didn't care about investments and such, but she thought the regular host of the show had a soothing and romantically manly voice.

Suddenly alert, she applied pressure to the breaks. Hearing Tony's voice on the radio had distracted her from driving, and the car ahead of her had stopped. After recovering from the her sudden stop, she listened as Tony critically analyzed the president's address.

"Of course him," she said to the radio. "He's the expert in all that is gloom and doom: 'prices rise as demand rises for a scarce resource' and all that eco-economic babble he was always spouting." However, she listened as he spelled out that just because Saudi Arabia's wells were dry didn't mean an immediate end to oil. The US had reserves and Canada had a large supply of oil-sand.

What was expected in the immediate was a rationing until the US could take stock in what was available around the county. Tony predicted that gas stations would re-open in the next few hours. Still, he warned that the days of paying $2.75 a gallon were over and to expect to prices upwards of $11.50. Then, in a couple of months, prices would near $25.00 per gallon.

The host of the show asked what listeners should be doing. Tony replied, "Right now, I would try to limit gas consumption and follow the president's suggestion: 'for emergencies only.' I would learn how to use public transit, and I would leave extra early as more and more people do the same in order to get to work and around to essential services. If you are physically fit, buy a bike today. Ride to work, feel the freedom that comes from moving under your own propulsion. If you are an investor and can afford it, get out of oil. If nations haven't already, they will nationalize petroleum in the next forty-eight to seventy-two hours. Then take your money and invest in renewables such as wind, hydro, and solar, especially solar. Solar is key to our future, and if you're not in solar, you've already lost."

The host thanked Tony for being on the show as Inez turned to take her exit. She thought, "He's going to listen to my message." After hearing him on the news, she was having second thoughts about their relationship. "Shit!" She said aloud to the radio.

She pulled into a gas station and parked. She called Tony.

The BP station was busy. People were driving up to the pumps, parking, and then driving away as they saw notes taped to each pump island. Inez thought that something similar must have been happening all over town as drivers tested the new reality of the day. She was sure that somewhere there was a riot. The nightly news would surely be full of horror stories and breaking news coverage from around the world. However, Inez was already looking forward to her mysteries. Today was falling apart, and it wasn't even noon. She had to get it together, and she wanted to start by trying to salvage something with Tony.

If Tony was planning to ask her to marry him in the next few days, she wanted to let him ask. It would be her first such proposal. Even if she didn't know how she'd respond today, she still wanted the romantic experience. She also wanted to see the ring. Tony had to have bought a ring, and Inez wasn't going to pass up the opportunity to see what he had picked out for her. Perhaps, if the diamond large enough, she would agree to be his wife. However, she still didn't believe he could live up to her domestic desires, but they'd never really talked finances. Maybe he was independently wealthy. She didn't know, but how could she find out before he asked her to marry him?

Tony picked up, "Yeah, Love."

"I just heard you on the radio on my way into work. I think you sounded handsome and intelligent." Inez then thought, "Good, he mustn't have gotten to his messages." Continuing aloud, "You want to get together for lunch or dinner tonight?"

"Are you okay?" He asked.

"Yeah. Why?"

"I got a strange message from you this morning, something about *needing something more*."

"I…"

"Don't worry. I think I know what you mean. I'm also looking for something more, and I'd like the chance to discuss what *more* could mean for us later. Yeah, I think dinner would work. My place or yours?"

"My place. I'll cook." Inez excitedly blurted.

"I'll be by around seven. I have a few more shows NPR wants taped today."

After they each said something less than "I love you," they hung up, and Inez collapsed over the car's steering wheel. Now, she was really late, and she hadn't called work yet. Her boss was going to kill her. Even though he liked her, he still expected her to be nothing less than perfect.

Thirteen

Everything was perfect. Inez had set a romantic table for two on her enclosed porch. The windows were slightly open. A light, cool breeze caused the candles to flicker and dance. The card table was covered with a white tablecloth that hung to the floor. She'd made the tablecloth specifically for a two person table, and across the top of the tablecloth Inez had stitched lace that hung off about a quarter of an inch. The place settings were red and yellow.

She'd decided to serve him a man's meal. She wanted him to see that she could prepare a hearty, but romantic meal. For Tony, she'd prepared a medium-rare one-and-half inch thick T-bone with sides of asparagus and a twice-baked potato. For herself, she'd prepared a small filet mignon to accompany the sides.

"It's ready." She said to the porch. Hugging herself, she ran into her bedroom to change out of her apron and jeans into something red to match the plates. Tonight, Tony was going to propose marriage. She wanted everything to be perfect. It wasn't every day that a woman's girlhood dream was fulfilled. Tony may not be a knightly man, but he was the man who was going to ask for her hand.

While she fluttered around the house, time seemed to slow and speed up and slow down again.

Fourteen

Tony finished his steak. "That was amazing." He chased the last bite with a swallow of wine. He looked at the wine glass and puckered his lips. "Well paired. Do you know a lot about wine? I just don't have the knack for it." He shrugged. "I don't drink much either. Coffee. Now, I know my coffees." He put the glass down and looked across the table.

"I'm glad everything went so well for you today. A book deal?" Inez smiled across the table and under it she ran her bare foot up Tony's leg to his knee. "I'm so proud of you."

"Ten years. Ten years, and it took a national, no, world disaster to publish it." He shook his head. "Did you see all those cars on the road today? I mean it was as if nothing has happened."

"We all had to work today. Maybe more folks will take you up on your bike and public transit suggestions tomorrow." She arched her back and pushed her chest forward as she sipped her wine. "I know I plan on riding tomorrow even though I have ample gas in the attic."

"Good. I'm glad to…" He stopped. "You have what in your attic?" He stood and walked around to Inez's side of the table.

"No," she thought, "propose here, on the porch." She stayed seated and looked up into his eyes.

"What did you say you had in your attic?"

Inez collapsed. Her shoulders rolled forward, and she pursed her lips. "Gas. I have gas in my attic."

"What do you mean?"

"A couple months ago, you told me that if the president ever said, 'Saudi Arabia lied,' I should go buy a stock pile. So, I did."

Tony bent over and kissed Inez hard on the mouth. "You're beautiful. How much did you buy?"

"Twenty four-gallon canisters and a mostly full tank for my car."

"Can I see them? And why the attic?" Tony started walking toward the door to the house. "Seems dangerous."

"I thought about that today." Inez tossed her yellow napkin on the white table, and it lay over both of the red plates. "Come on then."

"Have I upset you?" Tony asked.

"No. I just...the romantic moment."

"Oh." Tony looked embarrassed. "I'm bad with that." He walked away from the door. "Let's finish the wine."

"It's alright." Inez opened the door. "Perhaps, we can recapture the moment with dessert."

Fifteen

The attic was dark and hot. Without light from the sun though the attic window, they'd need to use flashlights. However, Inez never went into the attic at night. After they both had climbed the ladder, they waited for their eyes to adjust.

Tony had his arm around Inez. He said, "You know how I said I wanted to talk about what our relationship meant this afternoon?"

Inez couldn't believe it. The perfect scene was downstairs on the porch, and Tony was going to propose in the attic, hot and smelling like a leaky gas station. It was a nightmare that only a woman with girlish fantasies could dream, but she still wanted it badly. "You did say we'd talk."

They could see a little better. Moonlight or light from the street lamps turned the darkness into shades of complete black and light grey. Inez could see that Tony was down on one knee and reaching for her hand with his left. However, she couldn't make out was in his right hand, and she had to see it.

From the pocket seamlessly hidden in her dress, she pulled out the lighter she'd used to light the candles on the table. Holding the lighter in her right hand, she lit it with her thumb.

Suddenly, the room was full of light. The last image Inez saw was of a half-open red velvet box. Her last thought was that Tony had chosen wisely: The ring was large and amazingly beautiful. Then the world went dark in a thunderous explosion of refined fossilized sunlight.

Dogfight

"Give it up for the Fighting Bull, everyone." An announcer called. "The louder you chant, the harder she'll fight."

Inez Wick wondered at the torn skin stuck to her bloodied knuckles as she slumped into a dusty corner of the empty swimming pool. The calming silence that flooded over her after the gunfire signal to fight or be killed was still with her. Spasms quaked through Inez's bruised biceps. To the audience, Inez was a heroine, a modern gladiator. She was the crowd favorite, but the bookie's nightmare.

The crowd chanted, "Chicago."

Inez slowly got to her feet as the crowd's cheering flooded over her. The hair on her bare arms stood up. She tried to clean her hands off by twisting them in the loose fabric of the Chicago Bull's basketball jersey she'd been given to wear. The small pieces of flesh came off easily enough, but as the pulpy mess pealed away, Inez could see deep gashes in her own hands.

Inez grabbed a handful of blonde hair. The blonde couldn't have been more than sixteen or seventeen. She put her hand under the blonde's mouth. The blonde was still breathing.

As Inez put the blonde's head between her bare legs, she remembered her first win. How she'd cried like a little girl and begged for her opponent's life. Her first opponent had also been blonde, but her hair had been short like a boy's. The short hair had frightened Inez because it had made the other girl look tough, but the short-haired girl was weak and didn't put up much of a fight. Meanwhile, this one, this longhaired Barbie doll bitch, had been fierce.

Inez looked up. Her handler was talking to one of the other men that caught women for fighting. Her handler wore a driver's cap off to one side, while the man he talked to had a thin mustache. They exchanged a wad of money and her handler passed her thick white and rhinestone collar to the man with the thin mustache. She'd been traded, again. The price of victory seemed to include being bought by rich men. Rich men who'd use her for sex and fighting.

Inez held the blonde's head clenched between her knees. She ran her hand through the blonde's hair. Sharply, she twisted the blonde's neck, snapping it. Losing equaled death, and Inez wasn't ready to die.

Standing up, Inez pumped her fists in the air, shook her long black hair, and barked, howling victorious for another day.

No Compromise

The night sky was hazy. The stars tried to twinkle through, but the smog suffocated and dispersed their efforts to light the hillside.

"Dark is the night. These polluted shadows will be my cover."

Inez Wick checked her gear. Her black and grey calf high boots were secure and concealed a custom twelve inch blade attachment for the .44 Magnum holstered on her left hip. Combined, it was an odd and heavy weapon. Slow to load and prone to jam, Little Jon, as Inez referred to it, was more a liability than an asset. She kept it as a reminder that guns were a last resort, a tool of the desperate and underprepared. However, Inez ran her fingers over the barrel for reassurance before continuing her prayer of thanks, on bended knee.

"Mother, we have no divine right to subdue you. We are merely one of your many children. In your name, I reject even the notion of benevolent stewardship as that implies dominance. Guide my hand so that I may purge the sickness from you."

On her knee, she checked her air tank, thirty minutes. As she stood, she lifted the tank onto her back and secured her mask. Inez set her watch making sure to leave a five-minute window, which left her twenty-five minutes to get in, get the job done, and get out. Taking a couple of seconds to acclimate to the fresh clean O2, she thought, "No compromise in the defense of Mother Earth!"

While taking a few deep breaths, she opened the satchel that hung off her right hip, opposite Little Jon. Three explosive rods glowed like glam-girls at a rave party, eerie greens morphed into pinks and purples. Inez zipped the satchel shut.

High on pure O2, Inez ran down the hill. Withering brown trees, starved for sunlight, blurred together with the muddy soot laden soil. Dry leaves littered her path, but they made no sound as Inez's boots crushed them. Instead, the leaves turned quietly to ash and floated up a few inches into the air before returning to the ground, covering Inez's tracks perfectly.

Inez didn't slow as she approached the perimeter fence. Instead, she pulled a glowing ball, the size of a baseball, out of a hidden compartment in her vest. Inez quickly leaned into a hip-slide as she threw the orb. On impact, the orb popped. The fence sizzled and disappeared in time for her to slide through.

Once on the other side of the perimeter fence, Inez turned her slide back into a full run toward the nearest door. The gravel crunched and snapped underfoot, but no one noticed her. No one could see her. No one could see more than a few feet this close to the power plant, including Inez. She had to trust that her intelligence was correct, and that her trajectory was true.

She slammed headlong into a brick wall obscured by the smog. She let out a grunt as she collapsed to the ground. Her breather dropped from her mouth just as she was about inhale. Quickly, she replaced her mouthpiece before she sucked in the toxins around her.

Inez held still for a few seconds, recovering. She checked her shoulder, dislocated. Tears welled bellow her eyes, as she pulled her hand behind her body and wrenched up on it. She almost passed out, but knew failure wasn't an option. She had spent too much time and money on this mission. The largest coal fired power plant in China had to go off-line tonight.

The United Nations would meet in Beijing tomorrow. She needed the world stage to make her intentions known: polluters were targets.

"Mother, give me strength!"

Inez got to her feet. She couldn't see a door anywhere.

Probing the wall with her fingers, she slowly moved to her left. If she guessed wrong, the next door would be the front entrance, fully lit and guarded by nationalists. The light and guards mattered little, however. She didn't have enough clean O2 to make it that far around the plant. She'd suffocate about halfway around.

Feeling desperate, Inez took up Little Jon and attached his twelve-inch blade. In her left hand, she clenched a small flash grenade. Tense moments passed as she shuffled along the wall. Her watch told her that she had less than ten minutes of O2.

Just as Inez was about to admit defeat, she stumbled into a railing that led down into the ground. There were no lights. She listened. She heard nothing over the repetitive grinding of the coal processer. Inez thought, between the noise of the furnace and processer and the darkness enhanced by the smog, no one could see or hear her. Her caution was for naught. Taking a chance, Inez took out her mouthpiece and yelled in the din.

"For Mother!"

After replacing her breather, she felt stupid. The pure O2 must be affecting her judgment. Taking such a risk was beyond her talent. Shaking off her cocky compulsion, Inez followed the railing down into the belly of the beast.

At the end of the stairs, a deep red glow seeped out of an open doorway. At that moment, Inez realized her intelligence was faulty. The power plant was online. Her source had provided information that had led her to believe that the plant powered-down at night.

Inez looked at her watch. She only had minutes left. She'd wasted too much time already. She'd known that casualties were in the cards, but now, she wasn't looking at a few guards and nightshift drones. The plant employed several thousand when online.

Inside, the halls were filled with pipes, some carried steam, while others cold water from the nearby river. Upstream from the power plant, the river was clear. Downstream, the plant pumped toxic sludge into the water that poisoned and rendered the water unusable for a hundred miles.

Inez found the first attachment point. The cold-water intake was just down the hall. She'd recognized the intake from the drawings she procured from her source. She quickly set the explosive.

The second site was also easily reached. The underside of the furnace was hot. The air was so dry it sucked the moisture from Inez's clothes and exposed skin. The thin flesh on her slender fingers started to crack and bleed. The pain was intense and caused her to flinch as she placed the second charge.

The third and final charge presented a challenge. Inez looked at Little Jon.

"Looks like you're going to see some action."

Recovering the flash grenade from a pouch on her vest, she pulled the key and rolled it between the legs of two technicians watching the turbine slowly rotate generating the kinetic energy that would travel down power lines and into more than a million homes in and around Beijing.

The canister popped, blinding the technicians as Inez pushed Little Jon's blade in through the tech on the left's back. She turned the impaled technician to the right and pulled Little Jon's trigger. The bullet entered the technician's back and burst through his chest to fell the third and final technician.

Inez removed Little Jon from the technician and cleaned off the blade on his shirt.

Her watch was now ticking down the seconds until her O2 ran out. Inez knew she still had five minutes once the numbers stopped counting down, but Inez found little comfort in that knowledge.

She placed the final charge, and then she ran.

Inez knew that running would use up her O2 more quickly, but she had little choice in the matter now that all three charges were in place. The charges would sinc, which would mean they would detonate soon. She had to get clear of the immediate smog ring around the plant. The area would soon be a pit of fiery destruction.

As she ran, she held Little Jon out in front of her. She could see the stairs that had led her down into the plant. A technician sat smoking a cigarette on the bottom stair. As he looked up, Little Jon's blade slid into his right eye socket.

Inez didn't stop to see if the technician was dead. She kept running into the ring of smog. She knew that she'd have to deal with another section of the fence. She didn't have time to find the hole she'd made on the way in less than thirty minutes ago, and she didn't have anything to cut a new hole. She was going to have to scale the electric fence.

As she ran, she pulled out a pair of rubberized gloves and slippers. She pulled on the gloves and held out her hands in front of her just in time to stop her from being zapped. She quickly slipped the rubber slippers over her boots.

After a short climb, Inez started down the other side of the fence when the first explosion sounded. She let go of the fence and landed on the ground with a thud. Without thinking, she rolled up into a ball behind the first tree in the path of her retreat.

The second and third charge detonated. The force shook the earth, and rattled every tree on the hill. Fragile, paper-thin leaves fell slowly. A heat wave followed the shock sweeping up the leaves, before they could hit the ground, in a suffocating wind of poison.

Inez sucked hard on her O2 mouthpiece. She didn't have enough O2 left to escape. The forest around her blazed, orange and yellow flames jumped from tree to tree as if they were monkeys fleeing.

When Inez looked up through the burning canopies, tears ran down her cheeks. She could see the stars and the moon. The moon was only a sliver in the night sky, but that was okay. Inez couldn't remember the last time anyone had been able to see the moon in this part of China, and even if it was only a sliver, it was still beautiful.

Inez removed her breather and laid Little Jon beside her in the dirt. Coughing, Inez whispered.

"No compromise…"

Apophis

"More bars should be dimly lit and smoky." Inez Wick sat on the corner of the pool table, her pose suggestive. She held two fingers up to her lips. Then with an overdramatic flip of her long chestnut curls, she pretended to exhale smoky tendrils, giving the men in the room time to take in her long neck accented with large white hoop earrings and the plunging neckline of her tight blue sweater. "Don't you think?"

Janus racked nine balls. He pushed his glasses back up the bridge of his nose and ran his fingers through his short gray hair. Once the balls were properly aligned, the one-ball on the apex of the table, Janus removed the diamond shaped rack. "Your break." He replaced the rack under the table and collected his chalk and cue. He held the cue at eye level; it curved down and off to the left. "I understand your attraction to pool, but why this bar again?"

Inez pushed off from the table to collect her cue. She placed the cue ball in the bulk area within the D-line. Seemingly ignoring Janus' last comment, Inez quipped, "Everyone else in the bar is watching me…" She flipped her hair again and leaned over the table marking her angle. She stuck the cue ball, which squarely struck the one-ball. Following the laws of physics and mathematics, each of the nine balls traveled set paths that could be precisely predicted – that is if one was so inclined to prophesize such things. "…except you." Not a single ball dropped.

"You miscalculated." Janus smiled. "You never miss." He made his way around the table to the cue ball. "But you did put me behind the four and three balls. I don't have a shot." Janus put his hands up in surrender. "This must be the last bar that still allows…" He paused and looked around. A few patrons, a couple of tables over, were intently watching him. "…smoking."

"Then it's my ball in hand." As Inez picked up the cue ball, she patted Janus on the cheek, letting her hand slowly drift down his baby smooth face. "You ever thought about a beard, one of those short not-five-o'clock but not full-on caveman ones?" She set the cue ball down within the D-line.

Janus touched his cheek where Inez's hand had been. "Too much gray, people already think that I'm robbing the cradle." He looked into the mirror behind the bar and rubbed his chin. "What would you think of a mustache?"

"What kind?"

He touched his upper lip. "Einstein, Groucho Marx, or Zappa."

"Not Groucho Marx, but Einstein or Zappa would suit you." She put her index finger between her lower lip and point of her strong chin. "I could see a soul-patch."

Janus chuckled and slumped onto a stool. He looked at the table and whispered, "Nine balls. Nine planets. What if…"

Inez lined up the one-ball, "One, rail, far corner pocket." She took the shot: the cue struck the one-ball, and the one-ball followed her predicted path into the pocket, while the cue slowly rolled into the center of the felt. Moving around the table for her next shot, she asked, "What'd you say?"

"Thinking about *Apophis*."

"I brought you here to relax and forget about that 200 billion ton mass of iron and indium." She lined up the two, "Two, rail, my-side pocket." She taped the cue ball, which lightly struck the two-ball that obeyed her every word dropping into the pocket. "Is it the game?"

"What?"

"Pool!"

"The game." Janus rolled his head to the side. "Yes, sorry. I think that you've helped me, but not in the way you intended." He put the cue down on the table. He moved the three-ball to the foot-marker. "This is earth…"

"Can you give it a rest? You don't have to convince me. The proofs are mine: a 1 in 450 chance that *Apophis* will collide with one of our 40,000-plus satellites." She jumped back up to sit on the corner of the table and crossed her legs. She leaned back pointing her heels into the air. "You were going to lose."

"You always beat me." Janus finished moving the balls around the table. "Watch." He lined up the cue ball so that it would just miss the three-ball, Earth, but clip the seven positioned just off to the side. He struck the cue ball, which clipped the seven-ball pushing it out of orbit and into the corner pocket. The cue ball continued on its path, altered from the impact with the seven-ball, hitting the rail to bounce back out into space. On its return trip, after hitting another two rails, the cue ball lightly taped into the three-ball. "Ha!"

"What's your point? The math is sound: it's all just a matter of applied physics and geometry." Inez kept swinging her feet under the table and back up like a bored child. "And not one of our satellites is equal in mass to *Apophis*. Your little demonstration is not exact, a weak fear-inducing metaphor at best. You should leave that kind of nonsense to journalists."

"I want to look at the numbers again." He pulled on his coat. "I think that we need to account for the gravity of both the Sun and Jupiter."

"We haven't even eaten." She hung her head so that her curls bounced in front of her face, obscuring her sour expression. "Besides, my numbers accounted for the orbital pull from both the sun and *all* the other planets, including Jupiter. I even accounted for *Apophis'* passing by the cluster of planetoids beyond Pluto." Her tone changed from sweet and seductive into something monstrously terse, "It's covered."

He removed keys from his pocket. "I want to re-run the numbers." Janus started for the door. "I don't think that you missed anything, but I have a bad feeling that *Apophis'* orbit could alter several times, not just once." He looked up from his keys. "Besides, you're my student. If I allow you to turn in a substandard thesis to the committee, it degrades my credibility."

"Fuck you and your credibility." Inez shook her head. "I want to get something to eat." She flipped her hair out of her eyes. "Now, take me to that deli with the corned beef and sauerkraut sandwiches that you like so much." She jumped off the table.

"You know how genius works." He cocked his head to the side like a chicken hunting grasshoppers. "It's why I love you."

"Yes, yes; the work always comes first." She put on her coat. The fur-lined hood gave her a fuzzy plunging halo that turned even more heads than the sweater. "(Genius) = (Action) + (the Ability to Act)."

"And…"

"Fuck you."

"I'm sorry; I was doing it again: lecturing you." Janus pulled out his wallet. "Okay, let me settle up and then we'll get something to eat."

Inez watched him walk over to bar. She zipped up her coat and walked over to the far wall beyond the pool tables and big screen TVs to look at strange painting on the wall. It was a poster made to look like a painting of Goya's *Cronus Devouring His Children*. Bellow the painting was a display case of t-shits, beer mugs, and coasters with "Cronus" printed in purple block letters.

A brunet wearing a Cronus t-shirt and shorts that were shorter than her mid thigh apron quietly asked, "Get something for you?"

"A new thesis advisor." Inez reached inside her coat and adjusted her bra strap.

The waitress smiled. "You might not think he's into you, but he listened when you were talking. He seems to really care about your opinion." She looked out over the pool tables at the bar. "You're lucky."

"Lucky for now, until some new brain with bigger tits and a tighter ass comes along." Inez looked over her shoulder. "I know more than my fair share of 'smart men,' and they're only interested in you as long as your ideas are valid. God forbid," She looked up, "I...ah, I mean your calculations are inaccurate or proven false, or some other graduate student beats you to publication."

"I'm sure it's not like that. He..."

"I'll take one of those shirts." She looked up at the picture. "Do you know why I like this bar over every other pool hall in town?" She continued with out waiting. "I like the idea of Cronus eating his children: academics, like Janus, are very much like Cronus. They eat their graduate students and spit them out. They're all just a bunch of elite cannibals that feed off their intellectual children." She handed over a twenty and a five. "What's really sad is that they have an unlimited supply of eager students seeking to become just like them." She whispered, "Me included."

"I hope that you enjoy your new shirt and that we see you around here again." The waitress shut the drawer and walked in the back.

Inez looked at the shirt in her hand and then up at the painting. "Shit. So, then why do we play their game? Why do we let our ideas be eaten?"

Janus walked up behind her. "Because you can't resist Cronus' gray hair and good looks; besides, where else are you going to find a man who can truly appreciate your brilliance?" From behind, he wrapped his arms around her waist. He groped her ass with one hand and her left breast with the other. "Other men will only see your unquestionably desirable…umm, assets and be repelled by your intellect."

Inez pulled his arms tighter around her waist. "Fuck you." She spun in his arms to face him. She pulled his head to hers and kissed him hard on the mouth, and then pushed him away, leaving two red crescents on his lips. "Do you always have to go there?"

"Look. You're smart. You're in the top one percent. It sucks at the top of every mountain because there is nowhere left to go. So, what do we, the truly brilliant, do? We study Computational Astrophysics." Janus shrugged his shoulders. "You've doomed yourself to relationships with older men and cats."

"Cats?" Inez laughed.

"One day you'll wake up and have to ask yourself where all the damn cats came from, trust me." He put his elbow out for Inez to put her arm through. "You said you were hungry for corned beef?"

Inez took his arm. "Let's split the difference."

At the same time, they said, "Take out," and laughed leaning into each other. Lock-stepped, they walked through the sea of pool tables stopping occasionally to avoid drawn pool-cues like oars lifted from dark Mediterranean waters, intent on their coming action: a quick stroke converting human energy and innovation into directional motion.

"I'm more of a dog person," said Inez.

"Lucky for me."

Inez squeezed Janus' arm. "You know what I hate about you. I hate that you're right about me. I've tried dating other guys: meaty, sweaty ones who play sports and worry about missing 'The Game' on Sunday; the ones that want to know why I can't go to the club with them on Friday night, why I choose a lunar event over being his arm candy." She paused. "I want both worlds. I want a hunky guy that can bench-press his own weight and solve the mysteries of the universe with..."

"I do like this place." Janus interrupted and turned his head as he held the door for Inez to exit the pool hall.

"I know." Inez put a gloved hand to his cheek. "We'll come back again. Trust me." She took Janus' hand. "Let's go. I'm hungry, remember?"

Outside, Inez pulled her coat tightly around herself. Her stilettos clicked on the frozen asphalt parking lot. A light dusting of snow that drifted with each gust of the north wind obscured the white lines that usually guide cars into orderly stalls to maximize space. A few flakes swirled around Inez's head and landed on her cheeks and nose, in response she said, "Oooo! That's cold."

"You know you don't have to," Janus waved his gloved hand up and down as if he were one of Barker's Beauties presenting showcases on *The Price is Right*, "You know...all that for me. I mean really, it's..."

"Stop." Inez stood next to the passenger's side door with her hands on her hips and her feet planted as if she were going to charge him like an engaged bull. "A girl has to dress up once in a while. Those white lab coats do nothing for my figure, and I want to show it off while I still have it."

Janus opened the door for her and stepped quickly out of her way.

"It's not like you and I will be a thing forever. Enjoy what I have while I'm in your orbit because someday I'll slingshot right out of your galaxy." As she ducked into the car, she continued, "Think of me as your little comet: here today, gone tomorrow." She shut the door.

Janus made his way around the back of the car. He reached down to brush the snow off the taillights. He fumbled in his coat pocket, removed a small black velvet covered box, and held it in his hands. "You're wrong," he whispered. "You're my sun." He put the box back into his coat pocket and started to brush the snow off the windows with his gloved hand.

They drove in silence. The roads back into town were clogged with drivers too cautious to go more than the posted minimum. An eighteen-wheeler in the next lane over turned on its blinker, indicating that it wanted to merge into their lane. The blinkers running alongside the cab and trailer illuminated the snow-covered road like unwanted paparazzi flashbulbs exposing some lurid indecency. Janus eased up on the gas pedal. When the truck was out in front, Janus dimmed his lights then turned them back on. The truck pulled over in their lane.

Breaking the silence, Inez read aloud the interjection written on the back of the truck, "Explosively Crisp!" She crossed her arms, but a smile crept into her face, and she relaxed her shoulders, slumping into her seat. "I wonder what's in the truck," she asked.

Janus kept his focus on the road. "Honeycrisp Apples." He turned on his blinker and took the exit for 11th into downtown. The road curved, and he took 5th deeper into the towering wood of skyscrapers.

"Okay. I give up."

Janus' tone was flat with a hint of disappointed terseness. "As the truck pulled by, I saw the logo." He pulled over to the curb and put the car in park at a fifteen-minute meter. "Damn good apples."

"Okay Sherlock," Inez didn't move to unbuckle her seatbelt, "deduct what I want for dinner." Her pouting lips, fierce eyes, and tone spoke volumes.

Janus opened his door and step out of the car. He shut the car door with a purposeful soft click.

Inez slapped her hands on the dash. She opened her purse pulled out her cell phone. "Call Lab." She waited while the line rang.

"U of M, LCSE. How may I direct your call?"

"It's Inez Wick. Are the phones down again?" She bit down on her French tipped index finger.

"Yes. It is a scheduled event. The servers are being used to finish up an experiment."

She looked at her watch. It read 8 o'clock. "When will they be back up again?" She turned to look out her foggy window at the restaurant.

"Not until morning. Wait. Says here, not until 5am, and there is a note: 'I booked the full lab three months ago. So, fuck off! Sincerely, Dr. Steinborg.'"

"Thanks." Inez hung up. She unbuckled her seatbelt and got out of the car, and headed into the restaurant. She opened the door and walked purposefully over to where Janus was still waiting, hands folded in his lap, sitting next to the cashier.

Janus looked up. "I'm sorry. Here are the keys." He held out his keys. "I should have left the heat on for you."

"Dr. Steinborg reserved the entire lab until morning."

Janus put his keys back into his coat pocket. "Do you want to get a table?" He looked around the restaurant. "I'm sure we can get one."

Inez looked over her shoulder. "Sure." She dropped her purse in his lap, and walked off toward the washrooms.

Janus took her purse, walked over to the maître d', and asked, "Can I change my to-go order to eat here?"

The maître d' scanned his list. "This way please." He led Janus to a small table in back, near the door to the back-of-house. A buser hurried by with a blue tub of dishes reeking of garlic and sauerkraut. He brushed shoulders with Janus as he passed by. "Sorry, sir. This is all we have at the moment."

Janus took his coat off and hung it on the back of the chair closet to the isle. "Thank you. This will do." He sat and pulled up to the table. "Can I see a wine list?"

"Of course." He hurried off.

Janus fumbled in his coat pocket and pulled out the small velvet box and his cell phone. He flipped it open and dialed. He put the phone to his ear and waited.

"Janus, I booked the lab. Fuck off."

Janus' phone went silent. He put the small box back into his coat pocket and re-dialed. "Wait, wait. Please don't hang up."

"What? I'm in the middle of triangulating the…"

"I just need ten minutes."

"No."

"I'll take on one of your candidates."

"What? Why?"

"I just want ten minutes in the dome."

"Ten minutes and you'll take on one of my students, any student?"

Janus looked up at the ceiling. "I'll even take on that SETI freak. What's his name?"

"Erickson."

"Yeah, Erickson."

"Really?"

"Yes." Janus rolled his eyes and put a hand to his forehead.

"For Erickson."

"Yes. Hang on…" A waiter placed the wine list on the table in front of Janus and waited. Janus flipped it open and pointed at a $50.00 bottle of merlot. The waiter nodded and retreated. "I'm sorry about that."

"Yes, well, you called me. So, when, and how much of the server will you need?"

"When I get there. Maybe an hour or so from now. I won't need much, a gig maybe."

"Are you joking? Only a gig. What are you up to?"

"I need a couple of files that I've been working on. I want to use the projector and…"

"Spare me the details. You have a deal. Just call me when you need me to free up the processing power."

Janus clicked his phone shut and put it back in his pocket. He smiled and played with the velvet box in his coat pocket turning it around and around in his hand.

The waiter returned with the bottle of wine, presented it, opened it, and poured a tasting glass for Janus. Jan took the glass and swirled it around his nose and sipped. He nodded his head. The waiter left the bottle and two glasses.

Janus stood as Inez waked toward the table. He offered to take her coat, but she hung it on the back of her chair before sitting.

"Really, you don't have to take my coat and open doors for me. My father raised an independent woman."

"Spirited."

"No independent." Inez reached for the bottle of wine and poured a full glass, gulped half in single swallow, and wiped her lips with the back of her hand.

"Are you alright?"

Inez straightened her back and adjusted her breasts suggestively. "What are we doing tonight?"

"What do you mean?"

"After dinner, what are our plans?" She leaned in, putting her elbows on the table, hands outstretched to Janus.

Janus took her hands in his. "I've talked Steinborg down off the cliff. He agreed to let me use the observatory dome."

Inez took her hands back. She crossed her arms over her body, tucking her hands under her arms, wilting like a night blooming cereus flower at dawn.

"Don't." Janus reached for her hands. "It's not what you think."

"You really think my numbers are off, don't you?" She stood and reached for her coat. She held Janus in a death gaze. "And…"

"Please."

Inez leaded over. "See these." She pulled open the V of her sweater. "They wanted you tonight. They wanted you even after you ruined our game of pool, even after we left the bar." She straightened up and snorted. "They were even willing after they accepted they were going to be hidden behind a white lab coat."

Janus' eyes were wide. He looked like a beagle being sent to its kennel. He said nothing.

"I just don't understand you." She paused. "No, I understand you just fine. You." She shook her finger. "You are only concerned about your reputation." She stopped waving her hand when she saw the waiter arrive with their food. She looked around. Other guests were watching. She took her coat off again, put it back on to her chair, and sat down.

The waiter said, "Your corned beef and carrots." He turned to Janus. "Sir, your fish and chips." After setting down the plates, he hurried off.

Inez picked up the sandwich, dunked it in horseradish, and took a bite. Between chewing, "You're a lucky man."

"I know." Janus cut into the fish.

After finishing half her sandwich, she inspected Janus' plate. "What? We come here of all places, because you like corned beef, and you order fish."

"You like corned beef." Janus said lightly, putting down his fork, and dabbing at his lips with his napkin. "You are always transferring your likes on to me." He swallowed, and then quickly added, "Which is very endearing. It is one of the reasons I love you. If you didn't think that I liked so many things, I'd never leave the lab."

"You don't like corned beef?" She looked up from his plate. "You like fish and chips. I like corned beef. Why did I?" Inez looks off to the side. "I swear that when we were here last you had a corned beef sandwich and carrots."

"I don't care for cooked carrots." Janus picked up his fork and started working on another filet of fish. In between bites, he looked up from his plate. A furrow creased his forehead just above his bushy gray eyebrows. "You should finish your sandwich. You are always lamenting the leftovers: 'I can't toss 'em, they're too tasty; but they don't keep.'" He waved his fork. "So, eat."

Inez picked up her sandwich, "I sure do love this place, don't I?"

"You do."

They finished their food slowly, stealing quick glances at each other like mating birds during some elaborate courtship ritual. She'd finish her glass of wine and he'd quickly refill it. He'd begin to open his mouth to start up a conversation and she'd put a finger to his lips cutting him off. She'd smile and he'd smile.

Janus finished his fish and motioned for the check by holding up one hand palm up and signing it with the other. Their waiter hurried over with their bill, setting it down on Janus' side of the table along with a tray of brightly wrapped chocolate mints. Before their waiter could escape, Janus put a couple of bills into the folder and said, "Keep it."

They put on their coats. Their silent glances at each other, as they walked out hand in hand, they were tipsy and flirtatious, but they didn't say anything, letting wine induced emotions run between each other. Words would have only ruined the moment: one of them would have said something combative without intending it, which would have required, in their heated relationship, a quick rebuttal, and so it would go.

Janus opened the passenger's side door for Inez before colleting the tickets and folding them into a wad that he shoved into his pocket. He got into the car and started it.

"How many were there?"

Janus reached into his pocket and pulled out the wad. "I don't know. It doesn't really matter, does it?" He tossed them into the back seat, and he pulled a way from the curb.

"Where to now?" Inez drew the constellation of Three Sisters that make up Orion's Belt in the fog on her window. "We have the entire universe." She kicked off one of her heels and stretched her foot up onto the dash. She ran her hands down her leg. "Take me home and show me who's a Starship's Captain."

Janus turned the corner.

Inez pouted her lower lip and took her foot down off the dash. "You usually like my ship's captain come-ons." She turned to look out the window. "Not even a chuckle." Her voice was beginning to take on an angry edge. "You're taking us to the observatory, aren't you?"

Janus continued to look straight a head. He puckered his lips as if he had just tasted something bitter. "Yes."

Inez put her hands up to her face and shook her head. "Listen. You have a choice, and you're going to have to make it right now." She unzipped her coat and pushed up her breasts. "I'll lay it out for you like a multiple choice question: One. You take me home and fuck me like Jean Luc Picard up against the Borg. Two. You take me to the lab and we're through." She slumped back into her seat.

Janus kept his mouth shut. His brow creased as his knuckles turned white as he gripped the steering wheel. He dared to take quick glances out of the corner of his eyes.

"Really." Inez's mouth hung open. She puzzled with her nails, inspecting them for flaws and dirt. As she re-applied a shiny, clear lip-gloss, she stopped mid lip and turned to face Janus. "You. You're sleeping with someone else." She unlocked her door. "Pull over, I'm getting out." She opened the door.

Janus slowed the car but did not stop. He watched the passenger's side to make sure his door didn't collide with anything. "Inez, close the door," and in the same breath, "I'm not sleeping with anyone else." He quickly added, "I'm not seeing anyone else; there is only you."

"Then why?"

"I have something set up in the observatory that I want to show you." He let out a deep sigh. "I thought that using your numbers as a ploy to get you into the observatory was a good idea."

Inez shut the door.

"I wanted to surprise you." He pulled over to the curb. "I can take you home if you want, but I really want to show you what I've got set up."

Inez sucked air through her teeth. She uncrossed her legs and crossed them again, fidgeting uncomfortably. She waved her hand for him to proceed but did not say anything.

"Thank you."

Janus parked the car in the ramp. He quickly got out, rounded the car, and opened the door for Inez.

Inez took his hand and looked into his eyes. "Boys and their toys," she muttered.

They walked through the halls not looking at each other, standing the appropriate distance apart for an appropriate student teacher relationship. They stopped by Janus' office so that he could pick up his long white lab coat. They stopped by the student offices so that Inez could pick up her coat; she also changed shoes – out of stilettos and into sneakers with no-slip tread. To any causal observer, Dr. Janus and Inez were getting ready to study, ponder, and unravel the mathematical mysteries of the universe.

Except that Inez, who buttoned her coat up all the way to hide her out-on-the-town wear, didn't look particularly in the mood to solve mysteries. She looked cross as if she'd just found out that her cat shat in her Jimmy Choo leopard print booties. If she'd still been wearing her heels, as they walked down the tiled hall, the sexy click that tells a man a woman is approaching would have sounded more like gun fire.

Janus held the door for Inez and watched her stomp into the observatory. He tied a small black string on the handle, a known signal, which the male faculty developed long ago that meant *occupied.* He closed the door and locked it. While walking over to the computer, he called Dr. Steinborg. "Yes. Now."

"For Erickson?"

"Yes."

"Ha!" Dr. Steinborg hung up, but not before saying, "Sucker," under this breath.

Janus put his phone away and muttered, "I heard that."

Inez sat in the front row opposite the dome's controls. Her legs and arms crossed protectively as if bracing for an inevitable impact.

Janus felt the box in his pocket, and his smile returned brighter than a few minutes ago, brighter still than it had been in a long time. He pulled out a thumb drive from underneath his shirt on a dog tag styled necklace that he always had on around his neck. He inserted it into the USB drive and waited painful seconds while the computer recognized it. Opening a few folders, he came to a file named "The Proposal." He clicked on it twice in rapid succession.

The observatory started to dim as hundreds of laser-lights placed pinpoints on the inside of the dome.

Janus crossed the room to where Inez sat. He reached out his hand. "Quick, we only have a few seconds."

Inez took his hand. She looked at her watch, as Janus led her across the room. Next, she checked the star chart on her cell phone before looking up again. "The galaxy is out of sync. The North Star shouldn't be…"

"Stand right here." Janus looked at the floor. A black X in tape marked the spot where Inez was standing. "Here we go."

The stars started to slowly blur and bend down around the sides of the dome. Before Inez could ask or Janus reassure, the star-points rushed down around them, giving them the sensation that they were traveling faster than the speed of light.

Inez swooned.

"You okay."

"It's a bit much." Inez leaned into Janus embrace.

Janus steadied Inez in his arms. He took in the sweet lavender that she infused her hair with on occasion. "Just wait."

The star-points expanded and slowed as they passed by Jupiter, which filled the ceiling of the dome. They could see the massive storm twisting in its atmosphere. Then Jupiter too slipped by. However, their speed had slowed, and then it slowed some more as they passed by Uranus, Neptune, and Pluto.

Inez turned and said, "I still think it is sad."

"What?"

"Pluto being down graded to a dwarf planet."

"It's a plutoid."

"Yes, I know. It is now the name of a new class of planet or new class of asteroid, depending on whom you ask. I still don't have to like it."

They were into the outer asteroid belt now, and they stopped. The screen was filled with craterous potato shaped hunks of rock and iron. One large asteroid shifted on its axis as it spun not unlike a planet. As it slowly rotated it revealed a streaming light coming from behind like the headlight of an approaching motorcycle.

The screen shifted to the right and up. Then it backed up from represented reality to something that looked more like an orbital chart of the sun, its known eight planets, and Pluto. The head light became a comet with an elongated tail of ice and space dust.

Inez left Janus' arms and reached up as if she could touch it. She turned around and looked at Janus in the dim starlight. "Is it?"

"Yes."

"How?"

"I gave your data to Eugene, Dr. Rasome's computer modeling genius. I tell you, that boy is our future. We can crunch the numbers, but he can make it real."

Inez stood with her mouth open like a girl who'd just been given a pony for her birthday. She watched the asteroid travel her plotted path. She whispered, "*Apophis.*"

As *Apophis* punched its way through the asteroid belt it's trajectory altered ever so slightly. It then passed through the orbits of Pluto, Neptune, Uranus, and Saturn before entering into the gravitational pull of Jupiter. Jupiter's gravitational field pulled *Apophis* off course just enough to send it hurtling toward Earth.

Apophis approached Earth at breakneck speed. Suddenly, Earth filled the screen, and its fabricated satellites buzzed, clicked, beeped, and flashed tiny lights like a Christmas tree.

Inez watched as *Apophis* passed between the moon and Earth. She held her breath as it barely missed a British communications satellite before zipping back out into space to make its loop around the sun. As *Apophis* passed by the sun the program dimmed the dome lights before shining one lone spot light onto the floor where Janus was kneeling.

Janus held opened the small box. "Inez..."

Inez had quickly stepped over to Janus. She picked up the box and shut it. She handed it back to Janus and said, "No." She walked over to the light board and turned them all on. "Are you for real?"

Janus stood up and placed the box back into his pocket to hide his trembling hands. "I lov…"

"Stop." Inez stood by the door. "Just stop and think things through for a moment. You of all people should understand." She crossed her arms protectively. "You are always going on about your reputation, what the faculty would think, what the 'scientific community' would do." She used her hand to put "scientific community" in quotations. "Well, did you ever stop to think about my reputation? What I want?" She took a few steps forward. "I don't want to marry you. I want a career of my own. I want to be a respected astrophysicist in my own right." She paused to catch her breath. "What is it that you're always telling me: 'If you only shoot for the moon, you'll only land on the moon, and that's been done already. In order to succeed, you must pick and choose – very carefully – the things that you become attached to because attachments are weights, and if you are going to get anywhere, you must be weightless, and the heaviest weights in life are relationships: family, friends, and lovers.'" She paused and took a step back.

"I'm ready to be weighed down." Janus said meekly.

Inez wiped her eyes. "Well I'm not. I'm just getting started. I can't be weighed down."

"Then what am I to you?" Janus asked wide-eyed.

Inez looked astonished, eyes filling with tears again. "You're a means to an end." She wiped her nose. "Don't take that the wrong way. You're an amazing fuck, but that is what you are: an amazing fuck." Then she added, "And you're my thesis advisor." She cupped her hands over her mouth.

Janus smiled, and his eyes twinkled. "You'll be happy to know that I submitted your thesis to the defense committee earlier today, and I tentatively scheduled your orals for Tuesday. I know you're ready." Janus scratched the top of his head. "I must say that…"

"Shut up."

"Inez, I think that we can be adults about this and…"

"Shut up!" she yelled, and then as if cursing, she slurred out, "Shut up, shut up, shut up." Inez turned and ran out of the observatory.

Janus looked up at the sun, slightly obscured by the room's fluorescent lights. It hung there on the dome's ceiling, with a play-button blinking at the center.

Spilling Sunlight

One

Inez Wick watched the numbers on the gas pump. They flickered by faster than she could comprehend. The truck her father had given her for her sixteenth birthday, three weeks ago, had two tanks, twenty-gallons each. Gas was expensive, and Inez was learning the value of a dollar the hard way. At $2.89 a gallon, topping off both tanks cost $115.60. Along with the truck, her father had given her a credit card with her name on it. As she slid her credit card into the reader, she couldn't help but remember:

"Inez," her father was gearing up for one of his speeches, "pull over. I want to talk to you for a few minutes."

Inez eased off the gas and pulled off the highway onto the shoulder. Instinctively, she pulled the keys out of the ignition and put them into her purse. Then she set the emergency brake. Brushing her wispy chestnut hair out of her face, she turned to her father.

"That's my girl." He pulled at his mustache with his left hand and looked at his boots. "It's a nice day. Don't you think, a nice day to turn sixteen?"

"Sure, Dad." Inez pushed her sunglasses up, placing them on top of her head, revealing ice blue eyes, ringed and accented with light blue eye shadow and straight lashes caked with black mascara.

Picking his cap up off his knee, Inez's father opened the passenger's side door and got out of the truck. He had a lit cigarette between his lips before his feet hit the ground. He kicked a couple of rocks with the side of his boot. The rocks rolled down the steep embankment. The cattails were too thick to see where the rock went, but he heard them splash.

Inez stood beside her father. The warm southern breeze didn't provide much relief this time of year from the heat. Instead, the wind felt like a dog's tongue. The light summer dress was still too hot. Inez couldn't quite figure out how her father always looked cool in his long sleeve button-downs and blue jeans. When he'd caught her in Daisy-Dukes and a bikini top, he sat her down and discussed with her the difference between what a young lady wears and what a whore wears. He agreed to buy her short dresses with low cut tops and revealing backs, but he didn't want his little girl to look like the whores on TV or the ones that turned tricks at the truck stop just outside of town. She waited for him to say whatever was on his mind. She knew he was slow to speak and liked to choose his words.

After a second cigarette, he started in, "Inez, you know I love you." He didn't look at his daughter. Instead, he kept his eyes on the horizon. The sun was just starting to set and the last light of day was dancing in the marsh.

"I know." She thought he was talking about the truck. "I really like the truck, Daddy. You know I like red."

Her father smiled. "You're welcome. I know you'll get some use out of it." He shifted his weight. "I've been reassigned, sweetie."

It was her birthday. It was *her* day. One day, one day was all she asked from the world, a day where everything was beautiful and selfishly about only her. Keeping her composure by smoothing her dress, she asked, "Where this time?"

"Rig in the Gulf." He spat. "Just like last time, except this one's going to be deeper than the others. They want me to oversee the drilling."

"Alabama, Louisiana, or Texas?"

"Louisiana."

"How long will you be gone?" She knew the answer, but she wanted him to say it. She wanted him to know that he was

196

ruining her birthday – truck or no truck. If he left again, she'd have to stay with the neighbors, and the Halverson's oldest boy had a crush on her that made daily tasks like showering uncomfortable.

"Six months." He was on this fifth cigarette. "While I'm gone, I want you to have this." He handed her an envelope. "If you're old enough to drive, you're old enough to be responsible with one of those." He kicked another rock.

Inez opened the envelope. Inside, she discovered a blue plastic card. "A credit card?" She flipped it over couple of times studying it. Her name was printed on the front.

"Those are dangerous." Her father warned. "They're for emergencies and gassing up the truck." He stood over his daughter. "Listen closely, those things can ruin lives, but they're necessary. I'll pay for gas and emergencies, but anything else you'll have to pay for out of your allowance." He paused. "I want you to focus on school, but if you run up that card, you'll have to get a job."

Not wanting to change the subject, she pressed him about the new job, "Aren't there rigs off the coast here in Alabama?"

"Not new ones, sweetie." He let down the truck's tailgate and took a seat. "I drill. You know that. I go where they need drilling done." He motioned for her to sit on the tail with him. "Watch the sunset with me."

She didn't want to ask, but she needed to know, birthday or no birthday. Inez asked, "When?"

"Tomorrow morning."

Inez pressed the button on the pump for a receipt. Her father was big on receipts and had asked her to make a file for them so he could compare them against her credit card statements. She looked at the receipt. Her father worked for BP, and so he had asked her to gas up exclusively at BP pumps. She didn't understand her father's loyalty, gas was gas in her opinion. However, he had told her that BP was once called British Petroleum. Then it changed its name to Beyond Petroleum because it had been the first to break away from the petroleum lobby. Her daddy had said they'd planned to invest in renewable sources of energy. He had told her that of all the oil companies, BP was the only good guy, and he believed in supporting the good guys with his dollars and his labor. He might not work in renewables, but he wanted to leave that door open. However, Inez didn't see BP as a good guy because they sent her father all over the world to drill. All she wanted was her father home.

Inez was running late. She pocketed the receipt and jumped into the cab of the truck. She was picking up Kevin and they were going to the drive-in theater tonight, and she still needed to shower and freshen up. She made a mental note to call her father as they waited for the movies to start tonight.

Two

Michael Wick was covered in the black-ick. He didn't have time to worry about how he looked. He knew he looked like a sunburned raisin covered in chocolate syrup, but so did everyone else on the rig. He'd popped the well late in the night. The survey gear had suggested that where he was drilling was under an extreme amount of pressure. When Wick had suggested that they look for another angle, a new access point for the well, he'd been told to make do. The project had to say on schedule. Now, things were a mess, and all he could do was believe in his ability to control the situation.

Wick shot orders from the drill bit. His team of roughnecks was good at drilling, and he had handpicked each of them because they had experience containing blowouts. The depths at which they were drilling hadn't been tapped before and required precision. Wick expected mistakes and setbacks as they drilled, but he was confident that he and his team could handle anything,

Wick and his team needed only to drop the cement plugs because the primary cement fail safe had failed. Cement and sedimentary walls should have provided a significant buffer and prevented a blowout, but the well's casing had burst under the immense pressure. He hoped that the busted walls weren't too far-gone. If the walls were relatively sound, the plugs should seal the well. He'd sealed many wells before, but the pressure readings here were intense and getting worse as the crude erupted. Once tapped, a pocket like this one needed very little effort to extract. The pressure pushed the crude out with amazing force. Right now, he imagined that the flow was traveling about two hundred gallons a second.

"Mike!" shouted his boss, Ralph Gordon, "Mike, you gotta get that bitch capped. We're swimming in lost revenue." Gordon was a balding, sickly looking fat man who loved to chew on pencils. Even now, as he held an umbrella to shield himself from the spray, he had an unsharpened yellow number two between his teeth. "Lost revenue!"

Wick couldn't see Gordon and couldn't afford to look for him at the moment. He and two of his guys were leaning into a monkey wrench twice the size of man's leg that was attached to the pipe's connection to the docked tanker. As they pushed, the connection slowly clamped down. For now, the crude was funneling properly into the hold of the tanker, but he estimated that they'd lost more than 5,000 barrels. He'd stopped the immediate problem of crude raining from the pocket, but he still needed to cap the well or there was the potential for an even bigger problem.

He and his guys sat down, arms hanging loosely at their sides, chins resting on their chests. All said, it was a good day. He hadn't lost anyone, and any day he could say he hadn't lost anyone was a good day. For a second, he allowed his thoughts to drift to his daughter. He wondered what Inez was doing. He hoped that she was staying out of trouble this time. When Inez was younger, she liked to punish him by raising hell while he was on a job, but in the last couple of years, she had either mellowed out a little or just gotten better at hiding her mischief. Wick figured that their newly civil father-daughter relationship was likely a combination of love and respect, or at least that is what he wanted to believe.

One of the guys slapped Wick on the back. "Nice work." Cheers from the others brought a smile to Wick's leathery face.

Standing, he shouted, "Clean up this mess," before walking to control to see if he could salvage his tapping bonus. It was more likely that he was going to be fired and given severance. Then BP could save face. They'd look as if they were being proactive by placing blame on his shoulders. Accepting blame didn't really matter to Wick all that much, tapping was the most difficult part of extracting crude and lives were usually lost in the process. Publicly, he'd be slapped on the hand, but in six weeks he'd be on another rig searching for the sweet spot.

Opening the door, he confronted Gordon opened handed.

"Sit." Gordon quickly corrected himself, "No. You should stand. You're a mess."

"Sir." Wick waited, knowing how the conversation would play out. "I can explain. The…"

"Carlson has already informed me about the readings." Gordon rubbed his balding head and pulled at his shoulder as if he had severe back pain. "This wasn't your fault, and I need you to cap the well so that we can move on to a new location. So, don't pack your bags just yet."

Wick didn't know what to say. He'd been fired from every job he'd ever had. He'd made a fine living as BP's fall guy. The media needed one, and he was happy to take the fall, which meant extra vacation and extra time with Inez. Being fired and rehired was simply part of his job. Tapping oil deposits was messy, but as long as the demand for crude continued to increase, he'd be in demand. There were too few people willing to be demonized, so he had expected to be let go only to be rehired in a month or two. "You're not firing me?"

"No." Gordon dabbed at his forehead with handkerchief. "Carlson's readings indicate the pressure is still rising. Plug that hole."

"I'm on it. However, we might have to use the shears. Last I checked, the blowout in the cement walls let sea water seep into the drill."

"You're joking." Using the shears was a risky venture. It meant triggering sets of cams, near the wellhead, which should stop the flow by cutting into and sealing the pipe. The mechanism was simple enough and should work. "That's going to cost us the drill. We'll have to leave it on the ocean floor."

"It's better than the alternative."

"Before you do anything, go talk to Carlson." Gordon waved at the door.

Wick rushed out the door. As he made his way across the platform, he felt the phone in his pocket buzz. He pulled it out. It was Inez. He didn't have time, so he let her go to voice mail. When he had time next, he'd call her and catch up.

Carlson was pulling his hair, staring at readouts. He was muttering, "...not good, not good..." as Wick walked in.

"Jim." Wick and Carlson had worked the last five rigs together. Carlson's long graying blond hair hung off his shoulders.

"This is not good, Mike."

Wick looked at the readings. If the pipe were an artery, someone was having a heart attack. "We have to use the failsafe."

"No way, man." Carlson smacked the table with the palm of his hand. "That'll only increase pressure. Crude's moving faster than we can pump."

"The failsafe will stop it." Wick stood his ground. It was a risky move, but doing nothing was, well, doing nothing. "We don't have time. We need to seal it."

"You're making the call?"

"If you won't."

"I won't. Unlike you, I've never been fired. I've never had my picture in the paper." Carlson sneered, "And I don't plan on starting."

Without giving it another thought, Wick pushed the red, final fail-safe that would send the sheer rams into the pipe above the drill, capping it and rendering this tap useless. Wick looked at the readouts, they were still wrong. The pressure was still increasing. At first, he expected a higher reading, but the deposit, if capped correctly, should stabilize. The pressure should have evened out and become constant, however, the reading told Wick to prepare for the worst.

Sirens sounded. Lights flashed. Roughnecks secured themselves and tried to lay down on a flat surface. Then the entire platform started to buck like a skyscraper in an earthquake. Painful minutes passed as the rig danced like a kite in a strong wind. Everyone held on for dear life.

Carlson hugged the floor.

Wick did the only thing he could. He pulled down the radio. "Abandon rig. Abandon rig. Abandon rig."

Three

Inez Wick turned off her cell after trying to reach her father. He usually answered, even if just to tell her he'd call her back. She put her phone in her purse and tossed it behind the seat. The movie was about to start and she'd been ignoring Kevin's pawing.

To distract Kevin's probing fingers, as they danced up her leg, Inez undid her bra, pulled it out through the top of her dress and tossed it behind the seat with her purse. "No pinching, 'kay." She slid closer to Kevin across the bench seat, meeting him in the middle. The movie trailers and commercials for popcorn and soda were almost through. Their movie would begin soon. She'd convinced Kevin to see a romantic comedy followed by some eco-action flick about the end of the world, a movie for each of them, but right now she wanted action. She dropped the top of her dress off her shoulders and pulled Kevin's shirt up and off.

Kevin had lean muscles and pecs bigger than her boobs. He played soccer, and Inez had originally been attracted to his well-defined calf muscles and wavy hair. She'd seen him running laps with his team. He was the only one wearing glasses. Teasingly, Inez lightly twisted his left nipple with her right hand while biting his lower lip.

"Hey! You said, 'No pinching'." Kevin jerked back. "And you bit me." He might have sounded angry, but he didn't look upset.

"I want to see this movie." Inez pulled her dress back up and crossed her legs. "If you hold me like a gentleman during my film, I'll be nice to you during yours."

Kevin went to pull his shirt back on over his head.

Inez stopped him from putting his shirt back on, "No shirt." She flapped her lashes, took his shirt, and tossed it in the back with her bra and purse.

Kevin rested his arm on the back of the truck's bench seat. Inez moved in to the crook of his arm. He played with her hair and kissed her cheek.

After both of the movies, Inez was still wired. "Denny's?" she asked, pushing Kevin toward his side of the truck.

Kevin pulled out his phone and checked the time. He groaned. "It's almost two. You know how my mom gets."

Inez started the truck's engine. Looking over her shoulder, she backed out. "Does she still hate me?"

"She doesn't hate you." Kevin looked out his window into the darkness. "She likes you, but she hates your father."

"But she never looks at me. I can stand right next to you, and she'll talk about me as if I'm not there."

Kevin put his hand on Inez's knee.

Inez brushed it off, "Not while I'm driving."

"She doesn't like that he's an oilman." Kevin said. "I don't know what she means by it, but she keeps going on about how oil is really fossilized sunlight, the remains of dead plants and animals – dinosaurs. That oil will run out soon. And that burning fossil fuels is killing the planet."

"So she does hate me." Inez shifted in her seat. "You know, not everyone gets to pick what they do, sometimes it just happens."

"Hey! Why are you getting angry with me?"

"Because it sounds like you agree with her."

"I do agree with her." He looked out of the passenger window. He made a fist. Striking the door panel, he continued, "We shouldn't drill. The planet is sick."

Inez speed up, letting her emotions drive the truck. "It's not my father's fault."

"But it doesn't have anything to do with you, Inez."

"He's my father." Inez looked over at Kevin taking her eyes off the road for a second. "What if I told you that I think your mother is a dirty pot-smoking hippie that wants us all to live in caves, wear hemp, and eat berries. She's a freak – no one likes her."

Kevin looked away. Under his breath, he said, "Shut up."

"For God's sake, she even brings her own bags to the grocery store." Inez turned on the radio and started flipping channels. She didn't want to talk anymore. If she could have left Kevin on the side of the road, she would have.

Kevin slapped her hand and turned the radio off. "We're talking." He held her arm by the wrist. "When I'm talking, you'll listen."

"Kevin, let go. I'm driving." Inez pleaded.

Kevin pushed her hard. The truck swerved into the other lane, but Inez was able to keep it under control.

"Kevin, I'm done talking." Inez turned on the radio and set it to auto-flip channels. The radio played ten seconds and then flipped, Techno, Country, Top 40, Pop, News. While on the news station, Inez caught the words "oil rig accident." She quickly stopped the auto-flip, setting the radio to the current station.

Kevin interrupted, "Isn't Deepwater Horizon, the rig your dad is on?" He kicked the dash and smiled. "Serves him right."

Inez pulled the truck over. "Get out," she screamed. Her hair fell in front of her eyes. "Get out!"

As Kevin slid out of the truck, he said, "Play with fire, you'll get burned."

Four

Kevin's mother had earned her Ph.D. in Earth Systems from Stanford University. However, she was more of a hippie-activist than a hard-scientist, and she had imbued Kevin with as much ecological wisdom as his seventeen year-old mind could handle, which included as much guilt about being human as if he'd been raised a Catholic instead of an agonistic-humanist. On weekends, he and his mother would collect data in the low-lying wetlands that surrounded Mobile, Alabama. However, his mother's dream was to study Big Misale Bayou, which was one of the southernmost wetland areas in Louisiana. Kevin didn't know why she was so interested in Big Misale Bayou. She'd told him several times, but it was above his head. Before the spill, all Kevin had wanted, if asked, was to play soccer and make-out with girls. Now, all Kevin wanted was for his mother to stop going on news programs and riling up the neighbors. She was all talk and no action, always going-on about how people were destroying the earth, degrading natural capital, and having too many kids and overpopulating. Kevin knew she regretted having even one child.

On Saturday, he and Bill Hendrickson, his soccer team's goalie and his best friend, were bumming around the mall. The mall was small. It took up two city blocks, had a few chain fast food restaurants, clothing stores, and the only indoor movie theater in town. The theater had two screens, and Kevin thought both films playing were crap. The boys decided they'd head down to the beach despite the crowds to check out the oil. They'd heard that birds and fish were starting to wash up on the sand.

At the beach, Kevin spotted his mother surrounded by a media circus of cameras and clean-up volunteers. "Not again." He looked at Bill, "Let's go before it turns ugly."

Bill picked up a handful of sand and tossed it into the wind. "Not yet." He walked up behind the crowd. "Your Ma's preaching is always good for a laugh."

Kevin pushed Bill.

"Well, it's true," said Bill grinning ear to ear. "Now, shut up. I want to hear."

Kevin and Bill stood toward the back of the crowd, but they could hear Kevin's mother clearly. "...recover!" The crowd egged her on with cheers and threats of boycotting BP into the ground. "However," Kevin's mother continued, "And you might not like what I have to say next, but I feel compelled to say it: BP and the Obama administration are not the only conspirators in the spill." The crowd felt where the speech was going and there was an audible, collective grown. "Every one of us, if we drive a car, take a bus or a train, if we use electricity, plastics of any kind, paint our homes or seal our decks, buy food from nonlocal nonorganic farmers, we too must accept blame as end consumers. Our endless thirst for oil, our demand for cheap gas and petroleum-based products has placed undue pressure on the oil companies to extract crude, fossilized sunlight faster and cheaper." Someone in the crowd cursed. Another accused her of being a frigid bitch and a BP sympathizer.

"Let's go." Kevin pulled on Bill's shirt to get his attention. They walked down the beach a ways.

"No. I want to see this." Bill tried to stand his ground.

Kevin successfully pulled Bill away. "I'm not staying to watch. She calls it 'root out the cause,' but what it really means is making people feel bad for being human." Kevin looked out at the black water. Small rainbows danced over the slick surface. "Then the crowd will turn on her. She's so stupid sometimes."

Bill pulled out his phone, "I want to film it. Post it to one of those websites. You know the ones where bad stuff looks funny because it's not happening to you."

Kevin punched bill in the arm. "That's my mother."

"So what?" Bill tossed another handful of sand in the air as they walked away. "Hey, isn't that your girl, Inez?" He pointed down the beach. "She's still staying at our place. The news has been saying that the spill was her dad's fault, but no one knows for sure." Bill shoved Kevin. "You know, I bet she could use some southern comfort. Let her cry on your shoulder, 'Oh, Daddy, Daddy.' You let her do that, I'll bet you'll finally score with her."

Kevin pushed Bill out of his way and started marching through the sand. "Shut up. This is all her fault."

"Kevin?" Bill picked himself up and ran after Kevin.

Kevin had reached the spot where Inez was sitting in the grass. He kicked sand in her face. "You left me by the side of the road."

Inez's face was puffy and her hair windblown. It was obvious to anyone that she'd been crying. "Kevin," she pleaded.

"Look out there." Kevin pointed out to harbor. "Look at what your dad did." Without saying another word, he grabbed a handful of her hair at the nape of her neck. Picking her up, he slammed her face-first into the sand.

Inez tried to pick herself back up. Her head hurt. Her mouth was full of sand. A trickle of blood ran into her mouth. Then Kevin kicked her in the side, sending what breath she had left out of her lungs.

Kevin collected her in his arms. She was kicking and squirming, but she was little and light and he was strong. He took her to where the oily tide licked the beach. He tossed her into the slimy water.

Inez thrashed. Trying to stand was hard. She felt weighed down and her arms stuck to her sides. However, a few minutes later she'd found her way back on the beach. The tide still lapped at her feet, but she was free of the ooze.

"Bill, give me your lighter." However, Kevin was already searching Bill's pockets.

Bill tried to pull away, but Kevin had pushed him down again. "Kevin, what are you doing? Stop!"

Kevin found Bill's lighter. "Bill, film this."

"Help!" Bill screamed. "Help!" He ran off down the beach.

Kevin flicked the lighter to life and looked at the tiny flame flicker in the wind. Then he tossed the lighter towards Inez's oily matted hair.

Five

Inez ducked the lighter, which flew over her head and landed in the polluted water. The black sludge caught fire quickly like a butane soaked paper bag. Orange flames and thick suffocating black smoke spread in all directions. For a second, Inez watched the water burn.

While she watched, she thought of her father. He must have seen something similar before he died. He told her once that, despite the horror of burning crude on ocean waters, if you looked closely, you could see perfectly circular rainbows in the fiery mess. He'd told her that there was nothing more beautiful than a little spilled sunlight.

Then, as fear took hold of her, she started to stumble up the beach. Her clothes and skin matted down with the black stuff made moving difficult. It felt as if each movement would peel the skin from her bones. Despite the pain, she had to keep moving. The fire was chasing her, using her oily footprints in the sand, jumping from one to the next up the beach after her.

About The Cover Artist

Bob Lipski is the creator of
the comic book series "Uptown Girl".
His next book, 'Big City Secrets'
is due out spring 2011.

Bob lives in Saint Paul, Minnesota
with his lovely wife Amy
and their two children.

Visit uptowngirlcomic.com
for more information.

About The Author

Aaron M. Wilson was born and raised in Lincoln, Nebraska and now lives in Minneapolis, Minnesota. He earned his M.F.A in Writing from Hamline University located in St.Paul, MN.

He writes about books, stories, movies, and his experiences as an adjunct instructor of English, Literature, and Environmental Science on his blog: Soulless Machine. He also regularly updates Twitter @SoullessMachine.

His fiction has appeared in *eFiction Magazine: The Premier Internet Fiction Magazine, Evolve Journal,* Pow Fast *Flash* Fiction, *The Hive Mind, Eclectic Flash, Twin Cities: Cifiscape Vol. I, Girls with Guns Anthology,* and *The Last Man Anthology* – also featuring stories from Barry N. Malzberg, C.J Cherryh, and Ray Bradbury.

www.ingramcontent.com/pod-product-compliance
Lightning Source LLC
Chambersburg PA
CBHW050426260626
47156CB00003B/1173